Longing in Louisiana

Book Eight in At the Altar

by

Kirsten Osbourne

Prologue

Michelle Strempel hurried out to her car, smiling when she saw how clean it was. The students at Malloy High School, where she'd been principal for the past five years, loved her. Obviously they'd given her a surprise car wash. She could still see the soapy water trailing down the parking lot. She had never expected to be the popular principal, but she was. She loved her students almost as much as they loved her.

It was her rare night off from going to the sports activities of her students, and she was thankful for that. Four evenings per week, she went to some activity. She thanked God the district had decided Wednesday nights should be free for religious activities. It gave her a much-needed respite from ball games in the middle of the week.

She drove the six blocks through Malloy to the only restaurant in town, a small seafood place. When she arrived, she took a deep breath before getting out of her car. Her fiancé had asked her to join him for dinner, saying they had something serious to talk about when she'd told him she needed an evening at home. She didn't know what he had to say, but she'd gotten the impression whatever it was, she wasn't going to like it much.

She spotted his car parked two down from hers, so she got out and walked over, knocking on the window. "I'm here." She was too tired to even smile. Wednesday nights were for catching up on sleep. She preferred to see Bob only on the weekends. He took too much energy.

Bob looked at his watch. "You're fifteen minutes late."

She sighed. "I know. One of my students was having some trouble, so I waited with him until his mother arrived." The boy in question had been beaten during a visit to his father and hadn't wanted to be alone. She couldn't tell Bob that, though. Not only because of confidentiality, but also because Bob hated when she talked about work with him.

"Michelle, you can't let those children run your entire life."

Michelle shrugged. "I don't. I do care, though, and I was there for him."

Bob got out of his car without another word. "Let's eat then, shall we?" He seemed oddly formal, but Michelle tried not to be too worried about it. They were due to be married in mid-May, so they'd have the whole summer to get used to married life before she had to go back to her break-neck pace at work.

Once they were seated, Michelle pushed the menu away. She knew what she wanted. She'd eaten at this restaurant more times than she could count. A former student came to the table in a server's uniform. "Miss Strempel! It's good to see you."

Michelle smiled. The high school was small enough that she knew the names of every student who had graduated since she'd taken over as principal. "Brandi, how are you doing? How's the baby?"

Brandi had been pregnant when she'd graduated, and she'd fully expected to be kicked out of school when she started showing, but that was one of the first things Michelle had changed. She didn't think that girls should be kicked out of school for being pregnant if their equally responsible boyfriends weren't. How was that fair?

"Oh, she's great. Thanks for asking. She's walking now. Do you believe?"

Michelle smiled. "I'm always amazed to hear that children are getting older. Why, it seems to me you're still a freshman with braces on your teeth!" Brandi had always been a pretty little thing, and Michelle had been sad when the girl had to turn down the scholarships she'd been offered.

Brandi laughed. "I'm all grown up now, Miss Strempel. I'm married with a baby."

"Oh, I know. That doesn't mean I have to like it!"

"What do you want to drink? Sweet tea?" Brandi asked, looking at Michelle. She'd been in often enough that all the servers there knew her drink of choice.

Michelle nodded. "That sounds

wonderful."

"And you, Mr. Cooper?" Brandi's voice was a great deal more formal when she spoke to Bob.

Michelle and Bob had been engaged for three years, so all her students were familiar with him. For a while he'd even attended all of the games with her after school, but that had quickly fallen by the wayside. He'd claimed he had more important things to do than sit and cheer for a second-rate high school team.

"I'll have tea as well." Bob set his menu down.

"Sweet or unsweet."

"Sweet."

"Are you ready to order as well?" Brandi asked.

Bob nodded. "I'm ready if you are." At Michelle's nod, he continued. "I'll have the fried catfish. I want ranch on the salad and a baked potato loaded."

When Brandi looked at her, Michelle gave her order. "I want the grilled shrimp with grilled vegetables and no dressing on the salad." She had to make sure she fit into the wedding dress that was already hanging in her closet.

After Brandi walked away, Michelle gave her attention to Bob. "So what did you want to talk to me about? You're not adding more people to the guest list again, are you?" They'd been fighting over the guest list for months, and she was tired of trying to get every little detail just right. It was only two months until the wedding, but she was ready for it all to be over.

He unwrapped his silverware before placing the cloth napkin on his lap, his movements deliberate. Bob came from one of the wealthiest families in Baton Rouge, and sometimes he made her a bit crazy with how careful he always was about appearances. "No, it's not the guest list."

Michelle frowned when he wouldn't meet her eyes. "What is it then?"

He sighed. "There's no easy way to say this. My mistress is pregnant, and since it's a boy, I'm going to need to marry her and not you." His eyes were direct as he gave her his news, his voice as casual as if he was announcing that he'd just bought a new car.

"Wait, what?" How could he casually say that he was going to be a father as if she'd known for months about his mistress?

"Angela doesn't seem to be able to remember to take her birth control pills. The woman makes me absolutely crazy with that. She talked to my parents about the baby, and Mother says I have to marry her, or I'll be cut off." He rolled his eyes. "I'm sorry." His voice was too casual for her to believe his apology.

"How long have you been seeing Angela?" Michelle asked, doing her best to keep her voice down. It wouldn't be good for the principal to have a big argument with her fiancé in the middle of the only restaurant in town.

"Oh, five years? Something like that." He took a sip of the tea Brandi placed in front of him. "You didn't think I was going without just because you felt the need to be a virgin when you walked down the aisle, did you?"

Michelle wanted nothing more than to throw the contents of her tea into his face, but she held on to her temper. "I guess that would be too much to ask, wouldn't it?" She removed the sparkling diamond ring from her finger, and set it on the table, not willing to touch him as she handed it to him. "I hope you have a wonderful life with Angela."

"Life? Oh, I'll only stay married to her long enough to give the boy a name. We'll get married after that."

Michelle shook her head. "No, we won't. If you can't be faithful while we're engaged, then you'll never be faithful during marriage. I'm afraid this is the end of the road for us, Bob." She thought about storming out of the restaurant right then, but she couldn't. No, she'd let him pay for one last meal, and then she'd go.

She waited for the pain of her heart breaking, but truthfully, she didn't care about him enough for that. No, she was done with Bob. Forever.

Chapter One

Michelle sat back in her chair, rubbing her temples. She'd done something even she had never expected. The day after Bob had called off their engagement, she'd called a matchmaker. She had spent a lot of time and money on her wedding, and she was going to have it, gosh darn it! She didn't care what anyone said.

Dr. Lachele Simpson, the matchmaker, had made the trip to Tangipahoa Parish to interview her, and had promised she'd call by today. It was already past lunchtime, and even later where Dr. Lachele was in Manhattan. Perhaps she hadn't been able to find anyone for her. Maybe she'd determined that Michelle needed to spend the rest of her life alone.

She sighed. She had a honeymoon already planned, and she wanted to go. Of course, a week at Disney all alone wasn't something she wanted. Her students laughed at her for wanting to go to Disney World for her honeymoon, but she really didn't care. There was something about the giant rodent that made her smile, and smiling was something everyone should do on their honeymoon. Right?

She was startled when her cell phone rang. Looking at the display, she saw it was Dr. Lachele. She took a deep breath and swiped her finger across the screen. "Hello?"

"How does a wedding date of May twenty-first sound?"

Michelle smiled. It was going to work. "That's the date I already have a church booked for." She'd told Dr. Lachele that was her preference, of course. She had worried she'd have to try to switch everything, but Dr. Lachele had come through.

"Perfect. I'll be there, and so will your groom."

"And he's really willing to move to Louisiana?" Michelle asked.

"He is. He's self-employed, travels a lot for business, and he can have a home-base anywhere. He's happy to do it."

Michelle smiled at that. "What's his name?"

Dr. Lachele laughed. "You know as well as I do that I'm not going to tell you that."

Michelle grinned. She knew that one of Dr. Lachele's stipulations was that she wouldn't know his name until she met him—at the altar. She was going to meet her future husband in less than two weeks when she was walking down the aisle toward him. Better than being betrayed by a Bob.

"Sounds good. I'll see you at the church then."

"Email me the details, and I'll see you there."

"I have a honeymoon already planned for the following week. Make sure he doesn't try to book something for us. It's paid for."

"I'll tell him." There was a long pause before Dr. Lachele spoke again. "You're going to be happy, Michelle."

Michelle felt a tear trickle down her cheek. "I hope so."

"Trust me."

Michelle wasn't sure she'd ever trust anyone again.

Instead of calling off the wedding or telling anyone what had happened, she'd called Dr. Lachele to set up a match. It was ridiculous, and the craziest thing she'd ever done, but she wasn't about to spend the rest of her life alone. She'd become a teacher because she loved children. She was thirty-two. If she didn't get on the ball, she wouldn't have any. No, she was going to marry a stranger at the church where she'd planned to marry Bob. And she was going to be happy.

*****

Michelle paced back and forth in the bride's room at the back of the little church where she'd attended services since she was a baby. Her mother sat in a chair, looking at her worriedly. "You don't have to do this, Michelle."

"I don't have to, but I'm going to."

"But why?"

Michelle shook her head. She'd explained her reasoning over and over. She and Bob had started dating while he was in law school and she was in grad school. She immediately began teaching after graduation, and he'd started his career. They'd dated for six years before he'd proposed. She'd wasted nine years on a man who cheated on her. Nine years. She wasn't wasting another minute on a loser.

Michelle's sister, Alison, shook her head. "I think you should reconsider. No one marries a stranger. It's crazy!"

"As crazy as being in a relationship that lasts almost a decade with a man who is cheating over half that time? Is it the same level of crazy as that was?"

Alison sighed. "You didn't know he was cheating. You know you're marrying a stranger."

Michelle shrugged. "A stranger who has been matched to me, who an experienced matchmaker says will make me happy. Good enough."

"There's no reasoning with you!" her mother protested.

"Nope. I've made my decision, and I'm going to marry him. I don't care what anyone says."

The door opened then and Dr. Lachele slipped into the room. She seemed to assess the scene before her. "Michelle, are you ready?"

Michelle grinned at the woman in front of her. Dr. Lachele's hair was cropped short, and dyed a pretty shade of purple. She wore a suit that had the same shades of purple throughout. She even had purple heels on her feet. "I am. You look wonderful, Dr. Lachele."

The matchmaker cupped her breasts, pulling them up a little higher. "The girls do look good in this suit, don't they?"

At her mother's gasp, Michelle covered

her mouth with her hand, hiding her laughter. "I doubt they've ever looked better." She looked at her mom. "Mama, this is Dr. Lachele. She's the matchmaker I told you about. Dr. Lachele, this is my mother, Margaret Strempel."

Dr. Lachele crossed the room with her hand out. "It's nice to meet you, Mrs. Strempel. Your daughter has been a joy to work with."

When her mother simply stared at the hand in front of her, Michelle's gaze met Alison's, and she could see the amusement in her younger sister's eyes. "Do you have the flowers?" she asked.

Alison nodded. "The flowers are ready. Everything's ready. We have twenty minutes before the wedding."

Dr. Lachele turned from where her hand was still waiting to be shaken. "Your groom is here, and he's looking mighty fine today. I do love how a man looks in a tuxedo, don't you?"

Michelle nodded, not sure what else to say. She had no idea what her future husband would look like.

"Trust me. This man is going to knock your socks off." Dr. Lachele frowned. "Well, you're not wearing socks, but he's going to knock your garter off, for sure. He's one sexy man."

Michelle smiled. If he was sexy, it would certainly make her wedding night easier. She'd thought about asking him to wait, but she'd decided against it. She wanted babies as soon as possible, and she wasn't going to get them by putting off her wedding night. "Sounds good."

"He's a good man. In fact, he's one of the best men I've ever matched. He's moving here from Boston, and he's fine with a Disney honeymoon."

"Is he a Disney fan?"

Dr. Lachele shrugged. "He didn't say, but he said he'd be thrilled to go on a honeymoon anywhere."

Michelle blushed, thinking about all the honeymoon entailed. She was about to meet a stranger she'd be going to bed with that night. How on earth did you not blush when you thought about that? "I'm excited to meet him."

*****

Seth Henderson paced back and forth in the small room he'd been given to wait in until the wedding. His best friend, Daniel, stood watching him, obviously trying not to laugh. "I thought this was what you wanted!"

Seth frowned. "It is what I want. I just wish I knew more about her!"

"You know as much about your bride as I knew about Brenda on my wedding day, and look how that turned out!"

Seth smiled at that. It was Daniel's wedding to Brenda that had made him decide to contact Dr. Lachele. They were so happy together, and he wanted some of that happiness for himself. Who wouldn't? "It's different when it's me."

Brenda laughed. "I remember how nerve wracking it was to wait in the bride's room to marry a man I'd never met. I'm sure your bride is all freaked out right now."

Seth frowned at that. He didn't like the idea that his future wife was nervous about marrying him. "Well, how do I make her feel better about it?"

Brenda shrugged. "You don't. She won't feel better 'til she's seen you and talked to you."

"I wish I could make her feel good about it right now."

"But you can't," Daniel told him. "Just remember to always communicate. Text messages are fun."

Brenda blushed when he said that, making Seth wonder about their texting habits. "Text messages? Isn't it better to talk in person?"

Daniel shrugged. "You can't always be together in person. We couldn't at least. So text messages were a good substitute."

"I'll keep that in mind," Seth said, jerking when the door opened. "Dr. Lachele." He'd been surprised when he'd finally met the older woman. He had expected someone…well, someone a little less strange than what he found upon meeting her.

"You ready for this? Your bride is pacing around the bride's room like a crazy woman. Of course, she's perfectly calm compared to her mother."

Seth smiled at that. "I take it her mother doesn't approve?"

"Not one lick. Her father doesn't seem to mind, but her mother looks ready to jump out of her skin." Dr. Lachele walked toward him, reaching up to straighten his tie a bit. "I forget what a tall drink of water you are. Your poor bride is going to feel tiny in comparison."

"She's not tall?" he asked. He'd wanted someone just like Brenda, who wasn't even five feet, so he didn't expect someone tall. He just didn't know what to expect. Someone shorter than him certainly. At six-five, he'd rarely met a woman who was even within half a foot of his height.

Dr. Lachele shrugged. "She's about my height."

Seth nodded. Dr. Lachele was over a foot shorter than he was, so he was marrying someone who would feel tiny beside him. He had no preference either way, so he had no feelings about it, but it would make him feel protective of her. "What can you tell me about her?"

"I can tell you that she's going to be walking down the aisle in about three minutes, so it's time for you to get to the front of the church."

Seth grinned, having expected an answer like that. "Yes'm." He looked over at Daniel. "You ready to do this best man thing?"

"I suppose so. I don't really have a choice now, do I?"

Seth shook his head. "I wore a monkey suit for you, so you wear a monkey suit for me." Seth knew neither of them felt comfortable in a suit. They both preferred to wear jeans and T-shirts. They'd met in college more than a decade before, and Seth had worked for Daniel for a while. Now he owned his own business, but he was still frequently on Daniel's payroll. His internet security business was a necessity for an online matchmaking website like Daniel's.

Seth and Daniel strode to the front of the church while Brenda took a seat on the left side of the aisle. "I'm nervous." Seth hated that he felt so squirrelly about marrying a stranger, but he did. He trusted Dr. Lachele though, and that was what mattered.

"Deal with it." Daniel had his eyes on the back of the church as music started playing.

Seth's eyes were drawn to the huge doors at the back of the sanctuary. The woman he'd spend the rest of his life with would be walking through there at any moment.

When the door opened he felt his stomach drop. His new bride was the most beautiful thing he'd ever seen. Her long blond hair was swept back, and she had some kind of pink flower in her hair. Her wedding gown was strapless and cut to fit her perfectly. Her waist looked so tiny, he was sure he could easily fit his hands all the way around it.

She walked toward him slowly, her face solemn. He wanted to see her smile, but at that moment, it seemed to be taking all her concentration just to walk toward him. Her gaze met his and lingered.

She walked along on the arm of a man who had hair the same shade of blond as hers. The man kissed her cheek and put her hand into Seth's before turning to sit down beside a woman with dark hair and a grimace on her face. *That must be her mother.*

Seth looked down at the beautiful girl holding his hand and smiled, trying to let her know that he was excited and nervous as well, but he wasn't sure how to convey such a thing with just a smile. "Hi." The word was inadequate, and entirely inappropriate, but it seemed to fit.

"Hi," she whispered back, turning to face the preacher, but her eyes stayed on him. He knew because he couldn't keep his eyes off her. Maybe this would work out after all.

Michelle felt a calmness descend over her as she stood side by side with her groom. The words spoken by Pastor Franklin were familiar yet foreign all at once. She'd been told by many people that her wedding day would pass in a blur, and they were right. She wanted to stop and turn and talk to the man beside her, but she knew that Pastor Franklin wouldn't approve even if Dr. Lachele would let her get away with it. No, she'd have to get through the ceremony first.

Ten minutes later, the pastor's voice boomed out. "I now pronounce you man and wife. Seth, you may kiss your bride!"

Michelle hadn't thought about their first kiss being in front of all those people. She looked up at the huge man beside her. He was tall. So tall she felt like she was insignificant beside him. He reached out and caught her by the shoulders, pulling her to him.

Michelle tilted her head up, standing onto her tiptoes. She was barefoot under her wedding gown, because she'd always preferred bare feet. No one would see her feet under her gown anyway.

Seth smiled at her, leaning down and gently brushing his lips against hers. As soon as their lips touched, he felt a charge of electricity shoot through him. He'd felt passion before, of course, but never anything like he felt for his beautiful new bride. He wanted to stand there and go on kissing her, but he knew there were far too many people watching for that.

Michelle's eyes were wide when he lifted his head. It had been a chaste kiss. He hadn't tried to bring tongues into play. It had been a mere brushing of his lips against hers. So why had she felt so much from that simple kiss? She'd never had tingles spread through her belly when she'd kissed Bob. Seth had made her feel so many new things with a sweet kiss. She wanted to be alone with him. And soon. She wanted to talk to him. But more importantly, she wanted to kiss him again. And again.

He took her hand in his and turned to face the congregation. The pastor introduced them as Mr. and Mrs. Henderson, and he led her back down the aisle to the room at the back of the church where he'd waited for the wedding to start. "Do we have a minute before we have to go to the reception?" he asked.

She nodded, her eyes on his face. She was going to get a crick in her neck if she kept trying to look up at him this way. "The venue is just a couple of blocks from here."

"Sounds good." He took a step toward her, his hands going to her shoulders. "I—this is going to sound stupid, but I'm going to say it anyway. Kissing you was amazing. I have to do it again."

She smiled for the first time since he'd met her. "Oh?" She felt the same way he did. If she could bottle the feelings she'd gotten from kissing him, she would sell them and become a millionaire overnight.

He nodded. "So I'm going to do it again. Okay?"

His head was already descending as she nodded. Her hands rested on his biceps, feeling the strength through his suit coat. Her lips lifted to his, and she went on tiptoe again.

This time his kiss was more than just a gentle brush of lips against hers. He opened his mouth and slanted it across hers, demanding that she open for him as well. She moved closer to him, pressing her body against his. Her last coherent thought was that she could get drunk on his kisses, but then there were no thoughts at all as she was carried away by the passion of his kiss.

When he finally lifted his head, she took a step back, her breathing heavy and her heart beating rapidly in her chest. "Wow." It was the only thing she could say. She knew she sounded like a teenager, but all of her schooling went right out of her mind. She was a mass of emotions.

He grinned. "I couldn't have said it better myself." He sat down in a chair and pulled her down onto his lap. "I know I need to quit touching you, but I can't. I hope there's going to be dancing at this reception, because I need to have my hands on you."

She blushed even as she nodded. "Yes, there will be dancing. We're having chicken catered in, and we'll dance. The local country club is on a small lake, and that's where we'll have it."

"So your name is Michelle, right?" He laughed at himself. "I promise, I usually ask a woman's name before I start kissing her and pulling her onto my lap."

Michelle frowned. She didn't want to think about him with another woman on his lap. "Yes. And you're Seth?"

He nodded. "Yes. What do you do, Michelle?"

"I'm a high school principal. I started out as an English teacher, but now I'm in charge of the school here in Malloy."

"Really? You don't seem like the kind of

woman who would be able to be strict with kids."

"I rule with an iron rod…encased in velvet."

"So you're strong, but soft on the outside?" His fingers traced her cheek as he spoke. He really couldn't seem to stop touching her.

She nodded. "I love my job. I love my students. I work twelve hour days during the school year and sometimes longer, because I go to every game the students play in the evenings."

He nodded. "I've always worked long hours, so that won't bother me."

"The only evening I'll be home early will be Wednesdays, and that will be five instead of nine."

"I'll go to the games that I can. I'm in network security, and I travel a lot for work.

My home base has always been Boston, so I'll probably have to spend a lot of time in the Northeast until I've built up a clientele here."

"I'm off school until the first week of August, so I have some time to go with you or whatever. Dr. Lachele said you didn't mind a Disney World honeymoon?"

He shook his head. "Not at all. It honestly sounds fun."

"Have you ever been?"

"Nope. Never had that opportunity."

"You'll love it. I went once, when I was in college. Some friends and I went for spring break instead of joining in the debauchery that everyone we knew was part of."

"And that's when you decided you wanted to go there for your honeymoon?"

"Yes! I saw all the brides and grooms wearing their wedding veil and tuxedo mouse ears, and I knew I wanted to do that someday."

He laughed. "Well, if it's important to you, then I'll wear those mouse ears everywhere."

Bob had hated the idea of wearing the mouse ears, and it had taken everything she had to convince him to go to Disney World with her for their honeymoon. She was so pleased Seth was willing to do as she'd asked.

"Thank you. It really does mean a lot to me." She leaned over and brushed her lips against his once more. "We need to go to the reception."

He nodded. "I guess we do." He waited as she scrambled off his lap and stood up. "Let's go be newlyweds for a bit."

He held his hand out to her, and she took it, a smile on her lips. He was going to be a good husband. She could already tell.

Chapter Two

Michelle drove them to the reception, and she led Seth inside. She knew she'd have to tell him soon that he'd stepped into her wedding plans with another man, but her wedding day just didn't seem to be the time to tell him.

As they walked into the country club, Seth stopped short. "I'm amazed you were able to pull something like this together."

She smiled and kept walking. "Everyone's waiting on us to start dinner." She went to the table set aside for her and the wedding party. As soon as they were seated, the caterers brought out the chicken dishes she'd requested more than a year before.

At the table with them was her sister, her

brother-in-law, and two people she didn't know. "Seth, this is my sister, Alison, and my brother-in-law, John. Alison, John, this is Seth."

Seth smiled and nodded in greeting. "It's nice to meet you both." He turned to look at Michelle. "This is my best friend, Daniel, and his wife, Brenda. Dr. Lachele introduced them as well. My mom and twin brother couldn't make it today, so it's just us."

Michelle looked at Brenda. "I'm glad I'm not the only one who agreed to marry a total stranger."

Brenda smiled. "And she did a good job with Daniel and me. I have a good man."

"I'm glad. Tell me, do I have a good man?" Michelle asked as she cut a piece of chicken off from the grilled breast on her plate.

Brenda laughed. "No fair asking in front

of him! But yes, you have a wonderful man. Almost as good as mine." She pressed her cheek to Daniel's shoulder as she said the words, obviously in love with the man beside her.

Michelle watched the two of them together, enjoying their banter. She hoped that it wouldn't be long before she was that comfortable with Seth.

The talk around the table quickly became male dominated with the men talking about their jobs. John talked about his job as English professor at the local university, while Daniel talked about his matchmaking website.

"Why did you have Dr. Lachele set you up if you own your own matchmaking website?" Alison asked, a confused look on her face.

Daniel made a face. "Oh, I don't trust

computer matchmaking. I wanted the personal touch for my bride. I'm so glad I went the route I did."

"You don't trust your own company to do a good job?" Alison asked, surprised.

"I trust them with my income, but not with my heart." He brought Brenda's fingers to his lips. "Dr. Lachele did an amazing job, though."

Michelle looked back and forth between the other couple. "I'm glad to see a couple she's successfully matched."

Brenda grinned. "She also matched a friend of mine and her new husband. And a friend of hers. I know for a fact she's very good at what she does. Just make sure you give it time."

Michelle looked at Seth and found him watching her. "I think we're going to be just fine. I don't give up easily."

Alison nodded. "I can agree with that. She's the most tenacious woman I've ever met. Especially when it comes to her students."

After they'd finished the meal, they were called onto the dance floor to start the dancing. When Seth took her into his arms, she smiled. "Make sure you take tiny steps, or I'm going to fall."

He laughed. "I don't have much experience dancing, but I do know my legs are longer than yours. I'll be careful." His lips went to her ear. "How long do we have to stay here? I want to get you alone."

She shivered at the feel of his breath against her ear. "Not long. We'll dance a few dances, cut the cake, mingle a bit, and escape."

"Please tell me you want to be alone as much as I do."

She smiled at that. "Well, I'm nervous about tonight, but I want to be alone with you." Her hand which had been resting on his shoulder, stroked his face. "I'm surprised by how much I want to be alone with you." She'd expected to be going to bed with a man who she had no feelings for that evening, so she was pleasantly surprised to realize that while there was no love yet, there was plenty of lust.

He smiled at that. "I'm glad." He leaned down and kissed her softly. "When do we leave for Disney?"

"Tomorrow afternoon. I figured we should have our wedding night here before we rush off to the airport in New Orleans."

"Tell me about this area. How long have you lived here?" He really wasn't terribly interested at the moment, but he had to keep her talking so he could keep his mind off his hormones and talk of the wedding night would just make things worse for him.

"I've lived here my entire life. I grew up here in Malloy. I went to Southeastern Louisiana University in Hammond, which is about a twenty-minute drive from here. I lived on campus, but that's the only time I haven't lived in Malloy."

"Why didn't you commute if you were so close?"

She shrugged. "I had an honor's scholarship, so there was no need for me to commute. It was easier to live on campus and do the whole college student thing."

"Are you glad you did it that way?"

She nodded. "I am. I was very shy when I graduated from high school, and I'm not sure I'd have made friends on campus if I hadn't lived there. I'd probably still be having trouble talking to strangers." Many of the people attending her wedding were friends she'd made at Southeastern.

"How many people live in Malloy?" he asked.

"Only about three-thousand. The high school graduates less than thirty every year, which is just perfect in my opinion. I know every one of my students personally by the time they leave. I love my job."

He smiled at that. "I'm glad. I really will go to games with you as I can."

"I'm happy to travel with you this summer, and every other summer, if you'd like."

"You would?" He hadn't expected that from her.

She nodded. "Sure. I wanted to marry at the beginning of the summer so we could spend time getting to know each other until I go back to work. I couldn't do that if we were in different states."

"Sounds good to me." His hand stroked up and down her back. "How old are you?"

"Thirty-two. And I really want children," she blurted out. She hadn't meant to tell him so bluntly. "That's why I sought out Dr. Lachele. I feel like I'm getting too old to start a family, and I desperately want one."

Seth nodded, his eyes on hers. "I have no complaints. In fact, I look forward to making babies with you."

She blushed. "You really shouldn't say things like that in public. What if one of my students heard you?"

"Do you have students here?" he asked, surprised at the idea.

She nodded. "You know the girl who served our dinners? She's going to be a senior next year." She nodded at the boy who sat in the DJ booth. "That's Steven. He's going to be a junior."

"I'll watch my step then. And my tongue."

She smiled at that. "How 'bout you watch your step, and I'll watch your tongue."

He chuckled. "Now that's not fair. You can't talk about things like that if I can't."

"I made sure none of my students were close first. You didn't."

The song ended, and she danced with her father, and then her brother-in-law. Seth danced with her mother.

"You're going to be nice to my daughter, aren't you? You're not going to cheat on her?"

"No, ma'am. I'm not going to cheat on her, and yes ma'am, I'll be very nice to her. She seems like an amazing woman."

"She is. She's a good woman. She's a wonderful principal and an obedient daughter."

"I can see that." Seth felt uncomfortable dancing with her. He knew she must be worried for Michelle, though. "I will take good care of her."

"I hear you're going to go with her to Disney World for your honeymoon. Why anyone would go to Disney World for a honeymoon is beyond me."

"Because it's what she wants. If it makes her happy, I'm more than willing to do it."

"I don't want to like you, but you're making it very hard!"

Seth laughed. "I'm glad to hear that, Mrs. Strempel. I want to like you, though. And I very much like your daughter."

"I hope you still feel that way after a couple of months of marriage."

"Of course, I will." Seth couldn't imagine anything keeping him from liking the woman he'd married.

"We'll see."

When she said nothing else, Seth shrugged and kept dancing. He didn't know what the woman was thinking, and he wasn't going to question her too much. He didn't want anything to color his opinion of his new wife.

After he finished the dance with her mother, Seth and Michelle cut the cake. He carefully fed her the piece and found that he had frosting left on his fingers. She caught his hand and pulled it to her mouth, licking away the frosting that was left.

His eyes met hers and he felt his pants getting tighter. He wanted her in bed. Soon.

After they finished the cake, they talked to several of the people there. Michelle wasn't certain how quickly it would be all right to leave, but she was ready. At least she felt like she was ready.

Finally, her mother came to her and whispered, "No one can leave until you do. This would be a good time."

Michelle turned to Seth. "It's time for us to go," she said quietly. "Oh! I have to toss the bouquet."

She quickly tossed the bouquet out to a group of single women before taking his arm. "Mother said the gifts would be delivered to my house while we're out of town."

"How long are you planning for this trip?" he asked. "I only have seven days."

"I planned a week, so that's perfect. Where do you need to be in seven days?"

He sighed. "I have a trip to Boston a week from Monday."

"Well, that's perfect. I can go with you, or I can stay here and get all of your stuff put up."

He shrugged. "Why don't we play it by ear? See what we feel the need to do then?" Already he couldn't see himself leaving her when he left town, but he knew he'd have to once the school year started. Maybe it would be best if he got used to leaving her.

She drove them to her house, because he'd flown in. His car would be pulled behind a moving truck that wasn't expected until the day they got back from Disney. In the meantime, they would need to share her car.

When she pulled up in front of her house, she saw it through his eyes. It was a small white house, made of brick. It was a three bedroom two bath house, but only one story. She got out and opened the door, surprised her car hadn't been decorated. Maybe no one had thought it appropriate with the mess she'd been through since her engagement had been broken.

When she'd unlocked the front door, he scooped her into his arms and carried her inside. At her squeal, he laughed. "Didn't you expect to be carried over the threshold? Isn't that what a groom is supposed to do?"

"I guess I never really thought about it! I'm not used to being scooped up and carried anywhere."

He shut the front door with his foot and slowly lowered her to her feet. "Well, get used to it, because I kind of want to just stick you in my pocket and take you everywhere with me."

She laughed, shaking her head. "You can put that idea right out of your head. I'm used to standing on my own two feet, thank you *very* much!"

He looked around him, ignoring her, because he didn't plan on obeying her edict. "Nice house."

She smiled. "Thank you. I'm happy with it."

"C'mere."

She blushed. "I should probably get ready for bed."

"C'mere first."

She took the three steps that separated them, standing in front of him. "Yes?"

He pulled her to him, kissing her passionately, his mouth toying with hers. Within a moment, her arms wrapped around his neck, and she clung to him, unsure of whether her legs would support her.

When he lifted his head, he had a lusty look in his eyes and was pleased that she didn't seem to be able to stand. "You go get ready for bed now. I'm going to grab my stuff from your car."

He went out and got his suitcase, leaving her in the middle of the living room staring after him. She had a nightgown all picked out for her wedding night, and she knew she wanted to wear it. Hurrying into her room, she locked the door and changed into the frothy nightgown her co-workers had given her at a lingerie shower just before school had ended.

She felt incredibly uncertain about the night ahead. She'd been engaged for three years and had still never done more than kiss a man. Now she'd met this man just a few hours before, and he was about to take her to bed. What was she thinking?

Michelle sighed, thinking about the tall, strong, sexy man she'd just married, and she knew what she was thinking. She was thinking he was hot, and he was her husband. She had every right to want to make love with him, and more than that, she had every right not to feel embarrassed about it.

She may not be someone a man could

love, but at least she could tell he felt passion for her. It was something they could use to start building their relationship. Right?

Chapter Three

Seth brought his suitcase in and set it on the floor. He really didn't have anything he needed from it. He'd just wanted to give Michelle time to get herself ready for bed. He walked down the hallway, looking at the only closed door, wondering if he should knock or give her a little more time.

Deciding to err on the side of caution, he went to the kitchen and got himself a glass of water first. He leaned against the counter, sipping it slowly. How long did a man give a woman he had just met a few hours before to get ready for their wedding night? He wanted to laugh, because the whole situation was quite ridiculous, but it wasn't funny to him. She was the most beautiful woman he'd ever met. He just hoped she didn't come up with some reason to delay the wedding night.

He finished his water and placed the glass in the top rack of the dishwasher, amazed that the house was so clean. He wondered if she was a nervous cleaner. His mother had been, and every time something big was about to happen in her life, her house had been spotless.

He wandered to the closed door at the end of the hall and knocked, holding his breath as he waited for her to say something. She opened the door to him, wearing a silky white nightgown that ended at mid-thigh. He gulped, his Adam's apple jumping in his throat.

"You look incredible," he said, his voice a mere whisper.

"I feel silly," she admitted. "Wearing something like this for a man I just met a few hours ago is strange."

"So you'd wear it for a man not your husband?" he asked, knowing what she meant, but feeling the need to bait her anyway.

"I've never worn anything like this for anyone."

"Why not? You look beautiful in it."

"I—well, I've never done this before."

He blinked a couple of times, finally nodding. "You decided to wait for marriage, I guess?"

"Yes."

He took a step closer to her, not sure how to respond to the new information. "We're married."

She grinned at him, nodding. "Yes, I noticed that." She held up her hand that wore the ring he'd purchased for her. "You put a ring on it."

He looked down at her, trailing a hand down her arm. Her head didn't quite reach the top of his shoulder. He was almost afraid he was going to crush her when they made love. "Well, I did like it. Do you like the ring?"

"I do." It was a plain gold band, but it meant something to her.

"I thought we'd pick out an engagement ring together. I didn't know your taste."

She nodded, not really worried about engagement rings when she stood there in barely nothing in front of him. "That works."

He caught her shoulders in his hands and pulled her closer to him. "If we do too much kissing standing up, I'm going to get a crick in my neck."

She giggled. "I always knew I was short, but you make me feel tiny. How tall are you?" She'd always liked tall men, even though she felt dwarfed by them. Bob had only been about five and a half feet tall, and he'd had a short man complex.

"Six-five. Too tall?"

She shook her head. "I don't think men can *be* too tall!"

"But women can? Isn't that reverse sexism?" He stroked her cheek with his thumb, pulling her over to sit beside him on the bed so they'd be closer to the same level.

She shrugged. "I'm not super worried about being politically correct. This is a small Southern town, Seth. Things aren't quite like they are in Boston."

"I've kind of noticed that." Seth put his hand on the back of her neck and pulled her close to him. He still had to tilt his head to kiss her, even sitting, but it was better than standing. "I think I'm always going to kiss you sitting. Or better yet, lying down."

Michelle blushed. "I guess that makes

sense."

His lips covered hers, and his hands went to her back, molding her body to his. He wanted to pull her onto his lap, facing him, so they'd be at a better angle for kissing, but he wasn't sure how she'd handle that. After a moment, he decided to give it a try and pulled her astride him, never removing his lips from hers.

She pressed herself closer to him, loving the feel of his lips on hers. The man could kiss like nobody's business. She wanted to ask him how he got to be such a good kisser, but she really didn't want to know about past relationships, so she didn't.

She wrapped her arms around him, stroking him through the crisp white shirt he wore. He'd removed his suit jacket and left it somewhere, presumably in the living room. Where didn't matter a whole lot, though. She was just happy she had access to his body.

Most tall men she'd known were very lanky, with few muscles, but Seth must work out somehow. She could feel his bunched up muscles under his shirt. She pulled away from the kiss, her hands tackling the knot of his tie. "Do you work out?"

He nodded. "I run, and I row."

"I like the affect it has on you." She winked at him, surprised she could tease that way.

Seth laughed. "Oh, really?"

"Oh, yeah!"

"How 'bout you? Do you work out?"

She shrugged. "I sometimes run with my girls' track team."

"You do?"

She nodded. "It's a small school, with not enough coaches to go around. When the girls asked for a track team, I decided to coach it myself."

He shook his head. "I have a feeling you overextend yourself as much as I do."

"Probably, but I love my job and my students."

"I can understand that very well."

She threw his tie to the side and went to work on the buttons of his shirt. "It seems unfair that I'm practically naked, and you're still fully clothed," she said with a pout.

He laughed. "Is that what you're doing then? Making us more equal?"

She nodded, blushing again. "Of course it is. What else would I be doing?"

"I'm sure I wouldn't know." He loved watching her, thrilled again that she was the girl chosen for him. He needed to send Dr. Lachele a huge bouquet of flowers to thank her.

She pushed his shirt off his shoulders and

pushed it to the floor. "There. That's better." Her hands moved to knead the bare muscles of his shoulders. "I definitely like."

He grinned. "I'm not sure you're supposed to tell me that?"

"Well, I don't know any of the rules for this. I guess you'll have to teach me what I need to know."

"I like that idea." He pulled her toward him, kissing her again, his mouth more ravenous on hers than it had been. His hands stroked down the front of her, cupping her breasts in his hands. His thumbs finding her nipples through the silky fabric.

She gasped, pulling her mouth from his. "Why does that feel so deliciously naughty?"

"Deliciously naughty? I'll take that as a compliment!" He kissed a path down her neck and across her shoulder.

She tilted her head to one side, giving him

better access. "That feels so good!"

He caught her hips in his hands, pulling her closer to him so she was pressed up against his erection which was trying to drill a hole through his pants. "I'm not sure how much longer I can wait," he said against her lips.

She pulled away from him for a moment, looking into his eyes. "I don't think I told you to wait."

He smiled, pushing her off his lap, and standing before pulling the blankets back. He glanced over at her, wanting to memorize the picture she made standing there in her nightgown, her hair flowing down around her shoulders. "Have I mentioned how beautiful you are yet?"

She shook her head. "I'm so glad you think so." Bob had always acted as if she was lucky he paid any attention to her, and he'd been her first and only boyfriend. Having a man shower her with compliments of any kind was surprising.

"I do." He closed the curtain behind the bed, hating the thought of anyone looking in.

"That just looks out to the swamp behind my house. No one can see in," she told him.

He shrugged. "Doesn't matter. I want it closed."

"All right." She stood there awkwardly, wondering what he wanted her to do. She'd always thought that agreeing to have sex would be the hardest part, but really, she had no clue what she was supposed to do now that she had agreed.

He approached her, catching the hem of her nightgown in his hands and pulling it over her head. She blushed for a moment, wanting to cover herself. "You're not supposed to steal my nightgown!"

"Steal it? I'm not! It's not like I plan to wear it. I like it…but right now, I like it better on the floor."

She shook her head at him. "I had no idea you could act so—unruly!"

He laughed at that. "Unruly? Maybe I'll get sent to the principal's office, and you'll have to punish me."

She shook her head. "Behave!"

He pushed her onto the bed, following her down. His lips covered hers before she could tell him to do anything else. She was turning out to be a bossy little thing. When he touched her this time, it wasn't to explore, but instead he worked at bringing her to the same fever pitch he'd already attained. He wanted her to be just as ready for him as was possible.

He moved one hand down to stroke up the inside of her thigh, his fingers going to her core.

Michelle gasped as his hand touched her where no man had ever touched her before. She arched into his hand, her arms going around him and kissing him back passionately.

It wasn't long before he stood to remove his pants and covered her body with his. "Tell me if I crush you," he said, attempting to catch most of his weight with his elbows.

She shook her head. "You're not hurting me."

He leaned down to press his lips to hers, his hands stroking her body. "Are you ready for me?" he asked softly, even as he moved between her spread thighs.

"I think so." She wanted him, but she was nervous at the same time.

He reached a hand down to guide himself to her core, pressing inside. He pressed until he felt her barrier, and then, pressing his lips to hers to stifle her gasp of pain, he pressed hard, seating himself completely.

For a moment he lay still atop her, and then he slowly began moving. His hands never stopped stroking her and his lips stayed pressed to hers. He didn't want to hurt her, but he'd come too far to stop. The best he could do was make sure she finished before him.

When she arched beneath him, letting him know she'd reached fulfillment, he let himself go, finishing quickly. He rolled to her side and drew her close beside him, pillowing her head on his shoulder, his heart still pounding.

Michelle pressed a kiss to his shoulder, her eyes already drooping. It had been a long, exhausting day. Surely getting married did that to every bride. She was asleep within moments, leaving Seth awake to watch her sleep.

*****

Michelle woke early the following morning, as was her habit. She'd always been one to get up before the sun was up, simply because that's when her body woke her. She'd envied her roommates in college who could sleep until the alarm woke them.

She always woke up suddenly with full knowledge of everything around her, remembering what had happened vividly the night before. She slipped out of bed, looking back down at Seth for a moment before wandering into the bathroom to shower quickly. Their flight was at noon, so they didn't need to leave for the airport until nine or so.

She hurried into the kitchen to fix a quick breakfast, which she wanted to serve Seth in bed, hoping to brighten his first full day of marriage a bit. She couldn't believe the effect he had on her, and couldn't seem to stop smiling and blushing.

It was just after seven when she crept into her bedroom with a tray laden with breakfast for Seth. She sat on the edge of the bed, and reached out to wake him. When his eyes opened and met hers, she smiled. "I made you breakfast." She set the tray over his lap once he'd sat up, and went back to the kitchen for her own.

Seth looked at the feast in front of him. Michelle had made French toast, eggs, and bacon. There was a cup of coffee and a glass of orange juice as well. "You're spoiling me."

Michelle laughed, sliding back into bed beside him with her own tray. "Don't get used to it. Once school starts I won't have time for much."

"I guess I'll have to be happy with stolen moments during the school year."

She shrugged. "That's how it'll have to be. I'm sorry."

"No need to be sorry. I'll be wrapped up in my career as well."

"I do think I want to travel with you this summer." She couldn't believe it, but she already dreaded the time they'd have to spend apart once school started. She'd always been happy for a break from Bob.

He reached for her hand and squeezed it. "I'd like that a lot. We'll stay with Daniel and Brenda while we're there."

"Daniel was your best man, right?"

"Yeah. He's a good man. You'll like him." He shrugged. "He hit it really big with the business he started in college. You won't believe his house."

"A huge mansion?"

"Pretty much! I think Brenda is a bit overwhelmed by it still."

"I can imagine. She seems really sweet. Does she work?"

"She did customer service for a financial firm before they married, but now she just does volunteer work. She hated her job, and there's really no reason for her to work full time."

Michelle nodded. "If I hated my job, and you could support me, I wouldn't keep working either. But I love what I do. I hope you don't come to resent my job."

"What do you think you'll do after children start coming?"

She shrugged. "I'll probably put them in daycare or hire a nanny. I think I'd prefer a nanny if I could afford it."

"I'm sure we'll be able to manage that." Seth wasn't ready to talk about money much yet. He made good money, but relocating and starting a new business was hard. By the time children came around, he was certain they'd be well enough off to hire a nanny though. "When do you want to start trying for a baby?"

"Last night would be ideal," she said, not meeting his eyes. Had he thought she was on birth control?

Seth blinked a couple of times before nodding. "That's fine, I guess."

"I want two or three. I have never wanted to have an only child, and I'm already thirty-two. If I have a hard time getting pregnant, we won't have a lot of time for more."

He nodded, understanding her reasoning. "All right. We try right away then." Not that it was a hardship. He'd enjoy making the babies a great deal, and he'd always known he wanted children.

"Thank you."

"You're thanking me for doing something

I want to do. I mean, I've always liked kids and figured I'd have them someday, and really, it's no hardship to try to make them with you."

She blushed at that. "You really have trouble behaving, don't you?"

He shrugged. "It's just the two of us. No one to hear. I can say anything I want with my wife, as long as I'm not mean or rude, right?"

She nodded. "I guess so. Just don't make me blush all the time in public."

"I'll do my best. I may have a problem with that, though."

"What kind of problem?"

"I like to see you blush so much that I'm going to want to make it happen everywhere we go."

She shook her head at him. "How much do you need to do to pack for the trip?"

"I have no idea. There's never been any

time in my life for a Disney vacation. What do I need?"

She did her best not to gape at him. With as much as she loved Disney she felt sorry for anyone who had never gone. "Mostly just shorts and T-shirts are fine. Take some comfortable shoes. A couple pairs of jeans and nicer shirts for dinners."

"We won't just eat dinner in the parks?"

"Sometimes, but there are nicer places to eat as well. I have reservations for lunch and dinner set up for the whole time we're there. I hope you don't mind that, but some of the restaurants are almost impossible to get into. I love going to Be Our Guest at Magic Kingdom for dinner. I like to have my picture taken with the Beast."

"Do I get my picture taken with Belle then? Fair's fair."

"We can go hunt down Belle if you want,

but Beast is in the castle. Do you want to do the princess breakfast at Epcot? 'Cuz that's the easiest way to see Belle."

"Princess breakfast? I guess we could do that if you need to see the princesses."

"I don't. But if you want your picture with Belle, that's the easiest way to do it."

He sighed. "I guess I can skip a picture with Belle then. I don't know that I want to have breakfast with a bunch of screaming four-year-olds so I can get my picture with princesses."

She grinned. "I promise we won't be the only couple our age there without kids. You're going to love it!"

"Where are we staying?"

"I made reservations at the Wilderness Lodge on Disney property. It's a rustic place, and the restaurant there is really fun. I hear you need to ask for ketchup."

"Ketchup?" What was she getting him into?

"Yup. We're having dinner there tonight. You'll see."

He shook his head. At least she knew what Disney would be like, because he really had no clue at all.

Chapter Four

Once they'd landed at Disney, they took a private car to the Wilderness Lodge, instead of taking the free shuttle, which had been Michelle's initial plan. She didn't think Seth would appreciate the lack of leg room on the shuttle, though, so she opted for the more expensive option. For most men the leg room would have been uncomfortable. It would have been so much worse for her new husband. Seth wouldn't have had anywhere to put his long legs, though, and she was certain it would have been excruciatingly painful, trying to fold his legs up like a pretzel.

When they arrived at Wilderness Lodge and were welcomed home by the young lady stationed at the front, Michelle and Seth walked to the desk. She gave her name, and when the reservation didn't come up, she realized immediately what was wrong. "It's probably under Michelle Cooper."

Seth looked at her with surprise at the name, but didn't ask anything. Once they had their Magic Bands, they walked toward the elevator, following the little map they'd been given.

"Why was the reservation under Michelle Cooper?" he asked. "I thought your maiden name was Strempel."

She sighed. "It was." She knew she'd have to tell him, and it was obviously time. She didn't want to hide anything from him. She just wished she'd found the right opportunity to tell him before, because now it looked like she was being secretive. "I was engaged up until two months ago to a lawyer out of Baton Rouge. His name is Bob

Cooper."

"What happened?"

The elevator stopped on the second floor, and they walked toward their room. Once she'd opened the door, and they had their suitcases inside, she walked to the couch and patted the spot beside her. "He asked me to meet him for dinner on a Wednesday night in March, which was unusual. The district has made it so there are no sports games on Wednesday so the kids can go to church. Anyway, I met him at the only restaurant in Malloy."

"Okay…"

"He had something he needed to talk to me about. I assumed he was adding more people to the guest list again, but that's not what he needed at all. After we'd ordered, he told me his mistress is pregnant, and his parents were going to cut him off if he didn't marry her. He came from one of the wealthiest families in the state, and he wasn't willing to give up his inheritance." She shook her head. "He told me he'd just stay married to her for long enough to give the baby a name, and then he'd divorce her and marry me."

Seth blinked a couple of times. "Are you kidding me?"

"Nope. I told him that I wouldn't have him. I asked more questions, of course, and found out he'd been sleeping with her for over five years. He said I couldn't expect him to stay celibate just because I wanted to be a virgin when I married."

Seth shook his head. "That's crazy."

"What's crazy is I was in my town, in a restaurant where some of my former students work, and I couldn't throw my tea in his face and scream at him. I had to stay calm. I gave him his ring back, and I haven't seen him since. I called Dr. Lachele the next day."

He frowned. "So that's why you wanted to be married on that specific day? You already had the wedding planned?"

She nodded. "Yeah. I didn't see the need to lose all that money and all the time that had gone into wedding planning just because he was an idiot. So I married you on the day I was supposed to marry him. I know it probably wasn't the best way to handle things, but I couldn't see spending all that time all over again. I've been planning this wedding for three years!"

"I wish you'd told me."

"When? I met you at the altar! Was I supposed to tell you at our wedding reception? Or maybe while we made love? Or while we were eating breakfast in bed this morning? Oh, I know, I should have told you while we were on the plane flying toward our honeymoon."

He shook his head. "I don't know when, but you should have told me. Getting here and finding out I'm just a replacement husband is not the way I'd have liked to handle things."

Michelle sighed, taking his hand in hers. "If the situation had been more normal, I would have told you much sooner. It was just a strange way to meet and marry."

"I can understand that, but it still puts me in a very awkward position."

"Only if you want to let it."

"I feel like I'm filling in for him. Like you still care for him, and you only married me so you had someone to take his place." He shook his head. "I hate knowing that everyone you know went to a wedding expecting a different groom."

"That's not true at all. I had told everyone

there was a change of groom. Honestly, I don't know that I would have been able to go through with the wedding even if he hadn't been cheating on me. I didn't feel anything for him. Not sexually. I thought he was a decent man, and he's the only guy I've ever dated, but there was really nothing there. If I'd dated you instead of him, it would have been hard to wait until I was married. With him, it was just the easiest way to put him off."

"I need to think about it." He didn't know why he was so bothered by the fact that everything had been planned for another man, but he was.

She sighed, looked down at her hands in her lap. "I never meant to make you feel bad."

"I know you didn't. I just think you should have told me right away instead of making me wait. That wasn't a good way for me to find out."

"Tell me how to make it up to you, and I will. I promise."

He shrugged. "I'm going to survive. I just need to think about it for a while." He stood, walking toward the door. "I'm going to go for a quick walk."

She frowned, watching him leave. She hadn't meant to upset him, but she hadn't felt like she'd found the right time for her to tell him about Bob either. She pulled out her phone, punching in a number.

"Dr. Lachele."

"Hi, it's Michelle Strempel. I mean Henderson."

"Hi, Michelle! How's the honeymoon?"

Michelle felt tears prick her eyes at the question. She'd felt like everything was going so well, and then she'd blown it. "Well, I thought it was all good, but Seth is angry with me. I didn't tell him about my broken engagement, and when we checked into the hotel, I remembered that I'd booked it as Michelle Cooper, which would have been my married name if I'd gone through with my engagement."

"Uh oh. Did you apologize?"

"Of course I did! The timing just never felt right to tell him. 'Hi, I know we're married now, but I was engaged to someone else for three years, and this is our honeymoon we planned together.'"

"Yeah, that wouldn't have been good. I know where you're coming from, but you have to see it from his point of view as well. He thought everything was going great, and he gets thrown for a loop at the last minute."

Michelle sighed. "I know. What should I do?"

"You need to find a way to show him that

you're happy to be married to him, and not to Bob. A little sex wouldn't hurt. A whole lot of groveling might be good."

"But I really don't feel like I did anything wrong!" Michelle protested. "I would have told him when I found the right time."

"Well, sometimes being married means that you admit you're wrong, even when you're not sure if you are."

Michelle sighed. "If he ever comes back, I'll apologize again. And grovel. I can grovel when I need to." After hanging up the phone, she walked down to the gift shop on the first floor and bought the matching bride and groom mouse ears she wanted. They had dinner reservations at seven, so she hoped he'd be back before then. She thought about texting him, but realized she didn't even have the man's phone number yet. How odd to be married to a man and not have his phone number.

She unpacked for both of them, putting the clothes away. She'd gotten a suite with a living area and a bedroom which was separate. The bedroom had a king bed.

When she had everything in the room the way she wanted it, she sat down on the couch with a book and began reading. Her favorite thing about summer vacation was all the frivolous reading she could do. One of her roommates in college had gotten her addicted to romance novels, and she just didn't have time for them during the school year. It made her crazy not to be able to read whenever she wanted.

She glanced at the clock and realized it was after six and worried a bit about making their dinner reservations, but she figured she'd go alone if she needed to. At quarter 'til seven, he wandered back into the room.

She stood up and approached him, wrapping her arms around his waist, and feeling him stand rigid against her. "I'm so sorry."

"I think we just need to take the time to get to know each other better. We jumped into marriage as if it was a normal marriage, and I think we should take it slower than that."

Michelle nodded. "All right. If that's what you want." It wasn't what she wanted at all, but she wasn't going to argue with him. She was in the wrong, after all. "We have dinner reservations at seven."

He looked at the clock. "How long will it take to get where we're going?"

"Oh, it's here in the hotel." She grabbed her purse. "I bought our mouse ears, but we can wait to wear them if you want."

He shook his head. "No, that's something you've wanted to do for years. I'll wear the mouse ears."

She smiled, knowing they'd be all right if he was still worried about how she felt about little things like that. She went to get the Disney bag from the table and took out the ears with the tuxedo print and handed them to him. She put on the ears with the veil.

He grinned at her. He knew he shouldn't, but she just looked so adorable in the ears. "Those are sweet." He settled his own on his head, and turned to her. "No matter how upset I am with you, I think we need to present a united front. I don't want people to realize we're already having trouble on our honeymoon."

She sighed. "That makes sense. I'm sorry I upset you."

"I'll get over it. We're just going to take our time getting to know each other, even though we're doing everything backwards."

"What do you mean by taking our time getting to know each other?" She closed the door behind them and walked toward the elevator.

"I figured we'd sleep apart until we know each other better."

She blinked a few times. From what she'd heard all men cared about was sex, so why would he keep it from her, when that meant punishing himself? "Are you sure that's what you want?"

He nodded. "Yeah, I've been thinking about it. I think it would be best if we spent the week getting to know everything we can about each other and keeping sex out of it."

"All right." She was truly surprised that he would suggest such a thing, but if it's what he wanted, she wasn't going to argue about it. She'd enjoyed sex with him, but it wouldn't kill her to go without for a week. Maybe.

Seth frowned. She'd agreed a bit too readily for his tastes, but really what had he expected? That she'd beg him for sex? "So you won't mind sleeping on the couch while we're here?"

She wrinkled her nose at that. "We're both adults, and we're married. Surely we can find a way to share the bed without it causing problems."

He really didn't like that idea. He knew sleeping with her would be too tempting for him. "I think it would be better if you slept on the couch."

"Well, that couch doesn't seem like a comfortable place to sleep, and I think we can share the bed. If you're that determined, maybe you should sleep on the couch."

"There's no way I'd fit on the couch! You're shorter than me!"

"Yes, I am, but I also am not determined

that we need separate beds. You choose. We sleep together or you take the couch." Michelle stepped into the Whispering Canyon restaurant and gave her name. They were led to a table beside the windows which looked out over the impeccably manicured grounds. "There's a boat launch out there that will take us to Magic Kingdom or we can take the bus."

"Taking a boat sounds nice. What parks are you wanting to hit this week?" he asked, taking the change of subject in stride. They'd fight it out later if they needed to.

"I want to do Epcot, Magic Kingdom, and Animal Kingdom for sure. I'm fine with going to Hollywood Studios as well, but we only have six full days in the parks, because we fly back to Louisiana on Sunday."

Their server came to the table then and explained to them that if they wanted to join in the fun there, they should turn their card to the green side. If they wanted to just observe, they should choose the red. Michelle automatically put it on the green side, because she hoped it would help Seth out of his funk.

They ordered their drinks and the server came back with them a few moments later. After they'd placed their orders, she looked back at him. "I have reservations at different restaurants throughout the parks and the different resorts. I've been researching this trip for over two years."

"I'll just follow your lead then."

She nodded. "I thought we'd go to Magic Kingdom tomorrow. It's my favorite park. I have fast passes set up, but we can change them if you want. I just chose three rides that looked good to me."

He shrugged. "I really am up for anything. As far as I'm concerned, this is your special trip."

The meal was fun and the restaurant was boisterous. He enjoyed participating in the madness. After they'd eaten, she suggested a walk. "We can take the boat over to the campground from here and walk around there. It's really pretty."

He shrugged. It was getting late, but he didn't care. The only thing they had planned for the next week was playing in Disney parks. He didn't think he needed to be terribly alert for that.

They talked as they walked. "I was really shy when I went to college. I had a couple of close friends, but they went to other schools. The only thing I really excelled at was academics." Michelle knew he'd have had a hard time even talking to her when she first started school.

"So did you make friends easily once you got there?"

She shook her head. "Not at all. I took public speaking my first semester, hoping it would bring me out of my shell a bit, and it did. I made friends with my suite mates, and they gave me people to eat my meals with. It got easier as time went on, but my first semester was rough. My roommate was kind of nuts, and she tried to kill herself halfway through. So then I ended up rooming alone for the rest of the semester, but I slowly made friends."

"Did you start out as an education major, or did that change as you went along?" He held her hand as they walked along under the trees on the trails of the campground.

"Yeah, I was English education from day one. I never planned to go on for my masters, but I decided that I wanted to go into administration if I could. I started teaching as soon as I got my bachelors, and it was while I was doing my courses for my master's program that I met Bob."

"What was he like?" Seth found himself bristling as he heard the other man's name.

She shrugged. "I thought he was a great guy. He was in law school, and he came from a very different world than my middle-class background. We met on campus one day. He was throwing a Frisbee with friends, and I was studying under a tree. He tripped over my feet, and we talked for a long time that day. He took me to lunch, and we started dating."

"And you never had any clue he was cheating on you?"

Michelle shook her head. "We were both so busy. I was teaching English full time, while taking night classes and summer school. It wasn't until we were both out of school that we started to really get serious. He asked me to marry him shortly after I took the position of principal at my school."

"That was three years ago?"

She nodded. "He asked in September, so almost three years ago. I was so busy during the week that we only really saw each other on weekends. It never occurred to me that I should want to see him during the week. I was happy to only see him for a few hours on Saturday nights."

"Not even on Sundays?"

"No. I went to church on Sunday mornings, and Sunday afternoons were spent with my family. I really saw him on Saturday night and that was it."

"Why didn't you move in together?"

She shrugged. "I didn't want to sleep with him. I don't know. It just didn't seem right to me. So we stayed apart. I was content to keep him in his little compartment in my life. I was angry when he needed to see me on a

Wednesday night, because he didn't belong on Wednesday nights in my world. He was only on Saturday."

Seth shook his head. "It doesn't sound like you loved him at all."

"I don't think I did. I mean, he told me he loved me, so I said it back. I convinced myself he was what I wanted, but after we broke it off, all I felt was relief. I was happy to call Dr. Lachele, because it meant I had options."

"It really sounds like he meant almost nothing to you."

She nodded emphatically. "I don't know what I was thinking. I guess I thought that since he wanted to marry me he was the perfect man?" She shrugged. "I'm not disappointed that I didn't marry him." She stopped walking and turned to him on the trail. "I know you're going to find this hard to believe, but I already feel a lot more for you than I ever did for him. He wasn't the man I thought he was."

Seth stroked her cheek with the back of his hand. "I can believe that." He leaned down and gently brushed her lips with his, understanding better what her relationship with her former fiancé had been.

"What about you?" she asked. "Any skeletons in your closet?"

He turned around and started walking back toward the boat launch, knowing they would be sore if they kept walking. "Sure. You don't get to be in your thirties with no relationships. I had a long-term girlfriend in college. Her name was Shelly. We dated for three years. I figured I'd marry her someday, but we split right before graduation. She wanted to move to California to be a movie star."

Michelle grinned. "How'd that work for her?"

"I have no idea. I haven't seen her in any movies, though."

"Well, I'm glad she decided to be a movie star, because it meant she left you for me."

He laughed. "I guess she did. I went to see Dr. Lachele, because I felt like she'd done such a good job matching up Daniel and Brenda. I wanted a girl just like Brenda, but I think you're a whole lot more independent than Brenda could ever be."

"Probably. It's hard not to learn to be independent when you're running a school."

"Tell me about your school. How many students?"

She smiled as she talked about her job. "We have around one-hundred-twenty in the whole school. That's ninth through twelfth grades. The kids are great. I have very few discipline problems. It's more likely that the students will sneak and wash my car while I'm working late than one of them will vandalize something."

"No way! Your students really did that?"

She nodded. "They did. They do regularly. I know every single student by name. I get to school an hour before the first bell and I stand in the parking lot. I talk to every student as they come into school. When it's time for graduation, I make sure that I don't have to read a single student's name. It takes me about a month to learn all the new students' names when a new school year starts. They all know they can come to me with anything they need."

"That's really amazing. Would you ever consider moving to a bigger school?"

She shook her head. "I've been offered bigger schools already, but I'm content in

Malloy. My students love me, and I love them. The school is just the right size for me. It would be easier if I had an assistant principal to take on some of my work, but I don't. My staff is wonderful. The teachers are all dedicated to their jobs. I seriously have no complaints. Sure there are problems to resolve every school year, but I'm happy."

They got onto the boat to go back to the resort. "I'm glad. I've read that if your wife is happy, then it's easy to be happy yourself."

She clung to his hand. "I promise you, I am not keeping anything else a secret from you. Bob was the only thing I hadn't told you about, and I never meant for that to be a secret. I just hadn't found the right time to tell you yet."

"I can understand that." He brought her hand to his lips. "We'll work through it. We have the rest of our lives."

Chapter Five

When they got back to the room, Michelle went to change for bed. She wasn't sure exactly where she stood with Seth, but she felt like they'd made huge strides, so she changed into one of the skimpy nightgowns she'd been given at her lingerie shower.

Seth was already lounging in bed when Michelle stepped out of the bathroom, and he absently looked up from the mystery he had open on his lap. His eyes widened when he saw her standing beside the bed in a silky turquoise blue confection that made his heart beat faster. "I thought we were going to wait for a while before we explored that part of our relationship again." *And before I explored your body more. Definitely before that.*

Michelle tried to keep her face passive, feeling rejected. "This type of thing is all I brought to sleep in. It's my honeymoon after all. It's this or nothing." She shrugged.

He closed his eyes as she climbed into bed beside him. "I'm honestly not sure which is worse."

"Wow, Seth. Way to make me feel all sexy and attractive and stuff."

Once she was safely under the covers, he turned to face her, lying on his side. "I don't mean to make you feel undesirable. Having you dressed that way makes things a little harder for me." He grinned. "Okay, it makes some things a *lot* harder!"

She blushed when she caught his meaning. "You know, I think we could continue to get to know each other, even if we resumed our sexual relationship."

He shook his head. "I don't think that's a

good idea. I don't want how I see you to be clouded by the physical part of it."

"I feel like I'm the only new wife in the world who has to practically beg for sex."

He chuckled. "I haven't heard you beg yet, but it might manage to change my mind."

She wrinkled her nose. "Begging isn't exactly my style."

"Trust me, you won't need to. Just keep wearing that to bed, and I won't be able to keep my hands off you."

She put her hands flat on his bare chest, wondering what he'd worn to bed, but not bold enough to ask or look under the covers to see. "Do I get good night kisses at least?"

He frowned. "Maybe you should sleep fully clothed."

"I should be uncomfortable in bed, because you can't control your hormones when I don't want you to anyway? Not happening."

"Mr. Happy is going to be very frustrated by the end of the week."

"I know what would make Mr. Happy happy," she said, pulling him down for a kiss. She'd never been so bold with a man, but she'd never been married before either.

Seth couldn't resist her, immediately taking over the kiss. His arms went around her, and he pulled her close. He'd been crazy to think he could sleep in a bed with his new wife and not touch her. He didn't feel like he could back down though. His hands stroked her back as he deepened the kiss, his tongue tangling with hers.

Michelle's hands went to his back, and she ran her hands over the taut muscles there. He felt so good against her. She threaded the fingers of one hand through his hair, loving the feel of him.

He groaned and pulled away from her, rolling to his back. "We can't do that."

She sighed. "I like kissing you. Is that so wrong?"

"It's not wrong at all. I just—I know it seems stupid, but I really do want to wait a little bit. Please help me."

"Of course." She taught abstinence at school. She had to follow her own teachings. Walk the talk as it were. Of course, she didn't tell her students not to have sex after they married.

He caught her hand and brought it to his lips. "What time do we need to be at Magic Kingdom tomorrow?"

"I made lunch reservations for noon, and then we have three fast passes. We have dinner reservations at six in the park. I thought we could see what we wanted to ride between the fast passes. They won't keep us busy the whole time."

"What's your favorite ride at Magic Kingdom?" He carefully kept his eyes on the ceiling.

"Splashwater Falls, but I've heard amazing things about the new Seven Dwarves Mine Train. I can't wait to try it."

"Do we have fast passes for both?"

"Yeah. Splashwater Falls is right after lunch, because it's going to be hot, and I want to be wet when I walk around."

"Just don't wear a white T-shirt, or you just might kill me."

She giggled. "I could always go wet my nightgown!"

He turned to her with his eyes wide. "Are you trying to make me cry? Really? That's not very nice of you!"

She pressed her cheek against his shoulder. "Do I get to sleep in your arms? Or do I have to pretend there's a mini version of the Berlin Wall between us?"

He sighed. "I think for tonight we need to recreate the Berlin Wall with pillows. Lots and lots of pillows."

"You know, I thought our honeymoon was going to be a lot of fun. You sure are a party pooper." She moved to her own side of the bed and reached for some of the decorative pillows from the floor, arranging a wall between them. "There. Are you happy now?"

"Not particularly." He reached out and turned the knob on the lamp beside him and plunged the room into darkness. "And Mr. Happy is downright grumpy."

"Poor Mr. Happy…"

"Go to sleep, Michelle."

"G'night, Seth." She reached out a hand and held his over the wall.

"G'night."

*****

When Seth woke in the morning, Michelle was lying in bed on her stomach, reading a book. He watched her for a moment over the Berlin Wall. "What are you reading?"

"*How to Make a Man Want you in Six Easy Steps*." She continued staring at her book.

Seth closed his eyes. "You don't need any help on that front. What are you *really* reading?"

"Oh, a silly romance. I never have time to read them during the schoolyear, so I binge read them all summer long. Keeps me going."

"Is that one of those romances that has sexy parts?"

She grinned. "There are a few sexy spots. Why?"

"Wanna read me one?"

She looked at him, lifting an eyebrow. "I'm not sure you really want me to do that."

He sighed. "Probably not. Don't you feel like we know a lot more about each other after spending thirty-six hours with no sex?"

She shrugged. "I know how stubborn you are now, so sure."

"Stubborn, huh?"

She nodded. "Only a stubborn man would insist on the Berlin Wall in the middle of the bed on his honeymoon."

"Or one determined to get to know his bride better."

"Uh huh." She didn't take her eyes from the book.

"Are you angry with me?" he asked.

She shook her head. "Nope. Just reading my book. I want to see if they end up together at the end."

"Don't couples always end up together at

the end of romance novels?"

She shrugged. "That's what I hear. I haven't read them all yet, though, so I have to find out for myself."

"So are you planning on reading them all this week?" he asked.

She shook her head. "Oh, no. There are more published in a day than I could read all summer. I'll read a few this week, though. I had time scheduled in for sex, so if I'm not getting that, I might as well get my romance from somewhere."

Seth sighed and rolled out of bed, walking toward the bathroom in just his shorts he'd slept in. He felt her eyes on him as he left the room, and turned before closing the door. "Are you always going to watch me when I walk around mostly naked?"

She nodded. "It's my job as your wife to make you feel desirable."

"I see." He closed the door then, leaning back against it. Yesterday his plan had seemed so simple. Waiting to have sex again until after they knew one another better. She was making it very hard. In more ways than one.

*****

After a quick breakfast, Seth and Michelle took the boat over to the Magic Kingdom. "We can always take the bus as well, but I don't like the buses as much as the boats. It's also fun to take the monorail. We'll do that tomorrow when we go to Epcot."

Once they were in the park, Michelle smiled at him. "This is my place, and these are my people." She wore a pair of blue shorts that came to mid-thigh and a red tank top. He was thankful she hadn't worn white.

"What do you want to see first?" he asked.

"How would you feel about wandering down main street and looking in the shops? There's a little art shop up ahead that I adore."

"How do you know this place so well?"

She shrugged. "I told you I came when I was in college."

"Uh huh. How many times have you been since college?"

She grinned sheepishly. "I've been every summer. I love it here so much."

"You came alone?"

"No. I have a couple of friends who come with me, depending on the year. No one loves it quite like I do, but they're willing to humor me."

"Sounds good." He took her hand in his as they walked straight up Main Street. He was amazed at the detail in each of the buildings. He'd been to amusement parks before, because they were everywhere, but he'd never seen anything like Disney World.

The day was full of marvels for Seth, and the restaurant she'd chosen for supper was the perfect way to end it. They were seated in the West Wing, and he was truly impressed with the atmosphere. He remembered seeing *Beauty and the Beast* as a child, and loved how they'd turned the movie into a restaurant.

When he had the "gray stuff" for dessert, he wanted to ask what it was made of, but he couldn't help but worry that it would ruin the magic of the moment for him.

As they walked toward the front of the park, he shook his head. "This place really is amazing. I'm glad we came here." She looked so adorable walking ahead of him in her bride mouse ears that he had to grin.

She turned and looked over her shoulder at him with a huge smile as she wove through the crowd. "I'm glad you like it. Someday we'll bring our kids here."

"Absolutely." He adjusted his own mouse ears, hating how sweaty they made his head, but happy to wear them to please her.

When they reached the front gate, she turned to him. "We can take the boat back, or we can take the bus. Do you have a preference?"

"I'd probably rather keep taking the boat if you don't mind."

She shook her head. "I definitely prefer the boats, but I don't want to tell you how we have to spend our honeymoon."

"Today really was amazing. Thank you for all the planning you did to make it so special."

They headed down to the boat dock and she leaned against him in the line. "Why does a day of fun have to be so exhausting? My legs ache."

"I could give you a foot massage when we get back." The offer was past his lips before he could think about it. He really shouldn't touch her, and he knew it, but once the offer was out there, he couldn't take it back.

"That would be fabulous. I can return the favor when you're done."

He nodded. The only thing that sounded more torturous than touching her was her touching him. It was going to be a long night. "I'd like that."

They were on the boat as the sun set, and they watched it happen over the water. "So beautiful," she whispered, leaning her head against his shoulder.

He slipped his arm around her waist, supporting her. "I'm glad we had the day to share this, and I'm really happy I was there to see your face when you were first introduced to my favorite place on earth."

"We're going to be bringing our children here every year for the rest of our lives, aren't we?" he asked, a grin on his face.

"I can't think of a better place to take them. Can you?"

He didn't answer that, because he had no idea what it had cost for the whole trip. The cost of the meals so far had scared him a bit, and he couldn't help but wonder how she'd been able to afford to go there on a principal's salary. "I guess not."

She was dragging when they got off the boat at the back of the lodge. "My legs do not want to walk another step."

He laughed. "Mine are sore as well, but we'll make it. Maybe we should get massages. I'm sure there's a place to do that around here."

"Yeah, we could go to The Grand Floridian to their spa there if we wanted. I don't feel the need to spend the money, though. The whirlpool tub in our room is good enough for me."

He tried not to imagine her in the tub with bubbles up to her neck. "I'll have to try that as well then. I'm sure we can make it without the massage." He really was sore, though. He'd thought he was in good shape until he'd been asked to walk that much in one day. He didn't know how people did it.

When they got back to the room, she smiled sleepily. "I'm going to get in the tub if you don't mind. I need the magic of the hot water on my aching muscles." She knew from experience they'd be much worse the next day, but she hoped to keep them from getting terrible.

"Sounds good." He watched as she grabbed the romance novel she'd been reading and carried it into the bathroom with her. He settled down with his mystery and waited for her to make an appearance. He didn't even like to be separated from her when she bathed. He had it bad. What was it about her that was so special? He was already falling in love.

After her bath, Michelle realized she'd forgotten to take a nightgown into the bathroom with her, so she wrapped the towel around her, securing it with a knot just above her breast. Walking out of the bathroom into the bedroom, she dug through the top drawer to find something to wear.

Seth had his eyes on her from the moment she left the bathroom. "Are you trying to kill me?" he asked as she rummaged through the dresser drawer.

"Sorry. I forgot to take my nightgown in. I'll be decent in a second."

"No you won't. You're going to wear one

of those sexy little things again that are guaranteed to raise my blood pressure."

"If you don't like it, you're welcome to close your eyes. Or if you want, I can sleep in one of your T-shirts."

He shook his head. Seeing her in his clothes would be even worse, although he wasn't sure why. "No, wear the nightgown."

She disappeared into the bathroom with it in her hands and came back a minute later wearing a pretty pink nightgown that ended at the middle of her thighs. "You look so beautiful in those," he told her before he disappeared into the bathroom.

Michelle collapsed on her side of the bed, carefully forming the Berlin Wall with pillows again. She knew he didn't want to touch her, and she'd acquiesce to his wishes, even if she did think he was crazy. She opened her book and read, having finally reached the sex scene in the story. She didn't look up when she heard him come out of the bathroom, refusing to notice what he was wearing to bed. She wouldn't give him the pleasure of reacting to his nudity.

"Thanks for arranging the Berlin Wall," he said as he slipped between the covers. In truth, he wasn't sure why he was thanking her. He wanted to throw the pillows out of the way and make love with her. The fact that she'd obviously decided he was right and was willing to accept the sex moratorium made it that much worse in his head. What was wrong with him?

"No problem." She kept her eyes on her book, reading every word of the sexy scene.

"What are you reading?"

"Same thing I was reading this morning. Remember? The book on how to make your man want you in six easy steps."

"I'm going to look and see if there's really a book like that out there."

"You do that." She still refused to look up.

"Are you ready for sleep?"

She flipped through her book to find the end of her chapter. "Just six pages to go and I'm done for the night."

"I'll read a few pages then." He opened his book and stared at the words, not turning any pages, because he didn't really care what it said at all. All his attention was focused on her and what she was doing.

When she closed her book and set it on her nightstand, he closed his own, reaching out to shut off the light. "Aren't I even allowed to kiss you goodnight?" he asked.

"You were the one who enacted the Berlin Wall law. I was happy to sleep in your arms, but you said that it wasn't a good idea."

"Maybe I was wrong."

"Does that mean you want to remove the wall and sleep in each other's arms? Or does that mean you're ready to have sex again?"

He thought for a moment. "I'm not sure what it means." Running his fingers through his hair, he sighed with frustration. "I should probably just give up on my silly idea of not having sex. I mean, it's a crazy idea, right?"

She sighed. "I don't want you to go against what you've decided is best. If you want to make love, I'm all for it. If you want to lay here and pretend we're not married and have no feelings for each other, then we can do that too."

"What do *you* want? Truly?"

"Honestly? I want to make love with you. I wanted to make love with you last night. I don't think it's going to help us to withhold sex from each other. From what I hear, it's the best way to make up."

He grinned at that. "I've heard the same thing." He reached out and ran his hand down her arm. "And I have to admit, I do like to touch you."

"Really? I hadn't noticed." She grinned in the dark at his silliness.

She felt rather than saw him throw the pillows of the Berlin Wall to the floor before moving across the bed to take her into his arms. "I think this is the best thing for both of us."

She pressed her lips to his. "I'm sure it is. I mean, the Berlin Wall was such a hindrance."

"Definitely. No man should have walls between his wife and himself in bed. Even if they are made of pillows."

"I think you've made a very wise decision."

Seth smiled as his hands stroked over her

body. "I know I have."

She knew then he'd forgiven her for not telling him about Bob, and she was thankful. She didn't know how she'd have been able to keep acting as if everything was all right when it wasn't.

Chapter Six

The week of Michelle and Seth's honeymoon flew by. Before Michelle knew it, it was time to fly home to Louisiana. She always got sad when it was time to leave. Sure, she was ready to get back to her real life, but she hated to say goodbye to the magical world.

Once home, things would get a bit more complicated. They would only have two days at home, and then they had to fly to Boston. She definitely wanted to go with him and make the most of their summer together. She also wanted to get to know his friends and see where he'd spent his entire life.

When they arrived home on Sunday afternoon, they beat the moving truck with all of his things by about an hour. Michelle was working on getting the laundry going so they'd have clean clothes for their next trip when the moving truck got there, and she had to abandon her task to help get everything settled. He wouldn't need most of his furniture, and really there was no place for it, so she had the men put it into the garage while she went to work putting away his clothes and unpacking the boxes.

She was exhausted by the time they went to bed that night, and she settled against the pillows with a sigh. "That was a lot of work. Can we go back to Disney now?"

He looked over at her. "How often are you going to ask to go back to Disney?"

"Why? Does it bother you?" *If it does, I'm going to be bothering you a lot!*

"Not particularly. I'm just asking."

"Oh, probably every day or two for the

next seventy years. Is that too often?"

"I guess not..."

She moved across the bed and snuggled into his arms. "Thanks for humoring me and my Disney addiction."

"As long as you humor my addiction, I think we'll be good." He kissed her forehead, pulling her even closer.

She propped herself on one elbow looking down at him. "Oh? And what addiction is that?"

"You."

She shook her head but managed to catch herself before she argued with him. "That I can do!"

*****

They flew out Tuesday morning for Boston, and she was surprised at how nervous she was. They were in the air, and she was getting more nervous by the minute. "What if your friends and family hate me?"

He raised an eyebrow. "How could anyone hate you? They'll be thrilled that I care about you, and that'll be enough."

"I don't know. I've heard terrible things about mothers-in-law. Will she be mad we're not staying with her?" She was nervous enough about meeting her new mother-in-law that she wasn't sure how she'd handle it if she met an angry in-law.

"Not at all. She's downsized to a one-bedroom apartment since I went off to college. There's no room for us. She'd be the first to tell me to go stay with Daniel."

When he spoke about his mother, he had a slight grin on his face. She must mean more to him than he admitted. "How long has she been a single mom?" He'd mentioned once that it had been just him, his twin brother, and his mother most of his life.

"My dad died when I was ten, but she was a single mom for a long time before that."

"They divorced?"

He shook his head. "No, he was just never there. He had business trips every week, and he worked on the weekends too. He died of a stroke. I think he just worked so hard it finally killed him."

"That's really sad." She couldn't imagine losing either of her parents, and thankfully, they were both still very healthy.

"I never really knew him." He didn't want to continue on the subject, though, so he changed it. "I think you're going to love Brenda. I asked for someone just like her, and you're not just like her, but you're just right for me." He caught her hand and brought it to his lips.

She blushed. "Do you really think so?" She'd never felt like she was just right for anything or anyone. It was good to hear someone disagreed with her assessment of herself.

He nodded. "Truly. I can't imagine being happy with anyone else."

Michelle didn't comment on that, feeling that he must just be humoring her. She had always considered herself completely unlovable. She couldn't tell *him* that, though, so she changed the subject. "Tell me about her."

Seth looked at her for a moment before answering, trying to figure out what he'd said that bothered her. She got a look when she was upset, and she already had it. He couldn't imagine what he'd said or done wrong, though. "She's a caring little thing. Very family focused. She holds premature babies in a hospital as a community service."

"Oh, that's so sweet! I've heard about that and thought about it, but I'm so busy during the schoolyear that I want my free time during the summers. I guess I'm too selfish."

He shook his head. "You need to recharge during the summer so you can give so much of yourself during the schoolyear."

"You think?" She liked his theory, but she didn't know if he was right or not.

"I do. It sounds like you work so many hours that you practically run yourself into the ground. No one can keep up that kind of pace forever. Not even you."

She sighed. "I wish I could."

"I wish we all could. There's a reason God said to take the seventh day off. Working six days in a row is more than enough for anyone."

She nodded. "You're probably right."

"I hope I'm not too much extra to add to your schedule once August rolls around. I worry that I'll take up too much of your time."

"No way. I just hope I have enough time for you to give you the attention you deserve. If I don't, I'll make it up during the summers."

He laughed. "Are we both always going to want to give so much? This marriage thing isn't going to be too hard with the way we work together, is it?"

She shook her head. "Not at all. I hope we can both continue to put the other first. Of course, during school, I put my students first. That may mean staying late with a student in crisis. It will mean constant ball games and track meets and debate team meetings."

"I'll go to what I can with you. We'll have date nights with your school obligations."

She laughed, assuming he was joking.

"Yeah, we'll go to a high school football game instead of going to a nice restaurant. Who needs to go to a professional play when you can go to one put on by a high school of one-hundred twenty students! It'll be great."

"It sounds good to me!" He shook his head. "I don't think you understand how little I care about what we do as long as we get to spend time together."

"What did I ever do to deserve someone who would be so sweet to me?"

He grinned, touching her nose with his finger. "I think your students would have a long list of wonderful things you've done." The flight attendant stopped with the drink cart, interrupting their conversation.

"I think you may be right. They seem to have an over-inflated opinion of me," she said after the flight attendant had moved on. "Are you excited to be going home?"

He shrugged. "I haven't been gone all that long. I guess I'm excited to get to spend some time with my mom and with Daniel."

"Is Daniel picking us up from the airport?"

"Yeah. He said he and Brenda would both be there."

She knew the trip would be a quick one, because they were flying back on Saturday. "Are you working for Daniel on this trip?"

"That's part of why we're here. I have a job to do for Daniel's company, and there's a job with one of my old clients here. I don't see a need to get rid of any of the work I built up while I was here. I can always fly in for it. I'm not sure how much demand there will be for my work in Louisiana."

She shrugged. "We're less than an hour from New Orleans. I'm sure there will be a lot of work to do there."

"I guess I can start marketing there. I was going to try to concentrate in Hammond. Didn't you say there's a college there?" He'd prefer to drive a shorter distance to work in a smaller community.

"Yeah, I went to school there. I guess it's as good a place as any to start. Will you be renting an office? Or working out of one of the spare rooms?"

"Both of the spare rooms have beds. Would it be a problem for me to transform one of them into an office? It would save me some money."

"Not at all. We can move the bed out to the garage. I think I need to have a quick garage sale for all of our excess furniture anyway."

He nodded. "Most of my stuff consists of garage sale finds I got right after college anyway. I never really cared enough to spend a lot of money fixing up my apartment."

"That's what we'll do then." She rested her head on his shoulder. "Do you mind if I sleep for the rest of the flight? I'm tired."

He shook his head. He'd noticed already that flights tended to knock her out. "You sleep." He kissed the top of her head, watching as her eyes drifted closed. It was hard for him not to watch her sleep all the time, but he didn't want to be that kind of creepy guy. Of course, maybe husbands were allowed to be creepy.

*****

Daniel and Brenda met them at baggage claim, and Brenda hugged Michelle as soon as she saw her, while Seth and Daniel talked. "I'm so glad you came with Seth. I can't wait to get to know you better."

Michelle smiled. "I've heard a lot of really good things about you. Seth went to Dr.

Lachele asking for a wife just like you."

Brenda laughed at that. "Seth and I would drive each other crazy in the space of a week. No, he needs someone more independent than I am."

"You don't see yourself as independent?"

Brenda shrugged. "I guess I am, but I had no problem quitting my job and not working as soon as I got married."

"Well, from what I understand, there was no point at all in you working."

"Not financially, there wasn't, and I find I'm really happy doing volunteer work. I might even buy myself a little white tennis outfit and hang out at the country club all day hitting tennis balls."

Michelle laughed at the image that sprang to mind of Brenda doing just that. "Somehow, I can't see that happening."

Brenda wrinkled her nose. "It's not me at

all. I do not belong in the hoity-toity world of the rich and famous. At all."

"But you're there anyway."

"Nah. Daniel's rich. I just go with him when I have to and pretend I'm supposed to be there."

Michelle grinned at that. "Do you think Seth will go to school dances and hang on my arm like a decorative toy?"

Brenda giggled. "If he does, you have got to send me video. Daniel would never let him live it down."

"I might just do that."

The four of them walked out to Daniel's Lincoln Navigator together, and Daniel slid behind the wheel, while Brenda and Michelle got into the backseat. Seth frowned at Brenda. "Are you sure you don't want to sit in front?"

"Seth, my legs are a tad bit shorter than yours. There's no need for you to turn into a pretzel just so I can sit in the front. Besides, I'll enjoy talking to my new friend."

Michelle looked over at Brenda as Seth folded himself into the front seat, moving the seat back immediately. "You *are* rather short."

"Rather. Oh, well. I can wear heels anytime I want to. That's a plus, right?"

"I don't have a problem wearing heels. If I thought I was too tall for heels before, one look at Seth told me it would never again be a problem." She shrugged. "Of course, I've never felt like I was too tall for heels. I don't even think I'm average height."

Brenda nodded. "That man is tall. Like almost scary tall. It's got to hurt his neck to kiss you."

Michelle grinned. "It does! He makes me sit down with him." Or lie down, of course, but Brenda didn't need to hear about that.

Michelle was sure her new friend was fully aware of what she did with Seth anyway.

"I'm glad you guys are staying with us. We'll have to go shopping tomorrow." Brenda eyed Michelle. "Do you like to shop?"

Michelle shrugged. "I'm not a huge shopper, but there are some things I need. I'd like to get new school clothes this summer." She had budgeted a clothing allowance every month since she'd started working, and she'd barely touched it. It would be fun to use that clothing allowance now when she needed it.

"Perfect. We'll go into Boston tomorrow and do some shopping. And if you want, I can take you to do all the tourist stuff. I used to work at a little gift shop on the ocean walk in Plymouth. Plus there's loads to see in Boston if you're interested."

"Oh, so I could see Plymouth Rock? I guess I didn't realize it was so close to

Boston."

"Yes, it's not far at all. Would you like to go there? You could get something touristy and wear a lobster hat."

Michelle laughed at the idea. "My students would love to see a picture of me in a lobster hat when they come back to school in the fall."

Brenda grinned. "I'm sure they would! Do you have that kind of thing in your office?"

"I do! It's mostly Disney pictures, because I'm a huge Disney fan, but I get pictures wherever I go and put them up around the office. I have students coming in all the time to just say 'hi' and they wander around looking at everything."

"That's neat. I wish my principal had been that way in high school."

"Your school was probably too big for that. I only have one-hundred twenty students between four grades."

Brenda nodded. "Oh yeah. My graduating class was four times that."

"That's why it's easy for me to know each of my students personally. And they all know me."

"Sounds like you've got a good life going there, Mrs. Henderson."

Michelle frowned. "You know, I'm so used to being Miss Strempel, it's going to be weird to have to ask my students to call me something else."

"I guess you could keep Strempel as your professional name. I can't see Seth getting upset about that."

"I don't know about that. I can just change my name. It's no big deal."

"Are you sure? Because it seems like it is."

"Seth wanted someone just like you.

Would you have kept your maiden name?"

Brenda laughed. "Never. I was happy to change my name, but Seth didn't really want someone just like me."

"He's told me several times that you were what he was looking for when he went to talk to Dr. Lachele."

"He just thought I was what he wanted. Seth went to her so she could help him find the right woman for him. You suit him so much better than I ever would." Brenda looked down at her hands for a minute. "I don't know that I would have been able to deal with Seth. I'm happy with Daniel."

"Is there something I don't know about Seth that I should?" Michelle asked. "You're scaring me a bit here."

"No, there's nothing wrong with him. He's just...Seth never backs down from anything. Daniel and I mesh really well, but when Seth gets in his head that something should be a certain way, it better be that way. He's really rigid in his thinking sometimes."

Michelle nodded. "I've noticed that. And he gets the weirdest ideas in his head. Most hard-headed man I've ever met."

"You know what I mean then."

"I do. At least, I think I do."

They pulled up into the driveway then, and Michelle's eyes grew wide. Seth had warned her that Daniel had done very well for himself, and that he was a billionaire, but she was unprepared for the monstrosity of the home in front of them. "Wow."

Brenda laughed. "Imagine pulling up here for the first time and knowing you were going to live there."

"I can't!" Michelle had come from a solid middle-class family. They'd always lived in the same small town, always going to the same small church. She'd known few people out of her class. Even Bob's family had nothing on Daniel. "I've never seen anything like it."

"It's going to be fun having you here! We can swim and hang out in the garden."

"The yard is so big it has to be called a garden?"

"Well, of course."

Both of the women dissolved into giggles, causing Seth to look over his shoulder at them. "What's so funny?"

Michelle shook her head. "Nothing that would make sense to anyone else."

At her words, Brenda started laughing even harder, holding her side.

Daniel shrugged and looked over at Seth. "Women can be really strange."

"I see that."

Daniel parked the car and the men went to

the back to get the suitcases while Brenda led Michelle inside. "I picked the rose room for you."

"The rose room? Your rooms have names?"

Brenda bit her lip, fighting a laugh. "Yes, they do. Don't everyone's?" She climbed the stairs and led her new friend to a room at the back of the long hallway. "This one here. Last room on the right." Pushing open the door, she let Michelle precede her into the room.

Michelle walked in, looking around her. The bed was huge, and there was a private bathroom off of it. "Looks good to me, I guess."

"It seemed the perfect place for newlyweds. Way down the hall from us so you have a ton of privacy. No one will bother you."

"Thank you for letting us stay here. It's so

much nicer than a hotel, and I'll have a friend to hang out with," Michelle told Brenda, hugging her spontaneously. "I really do appreciate it."

"We're so happy to have you. I hope you thought to bring a swim suit, but if you didn't, we can get one while we're shopping tomorrow."

"Seth told me I'd probably need one, so I brought two."

"Perfect," Brenda said. "We'll go hang out in the pool after supper."

On cue, Michelle's stomach rumbled. "I do hope it's soon," she said with a laugh.

"Oh, it is. Mrs. Brinkley always cooks delicious stuff. And it's always ready at precisely six in the evening. It's five 'til now."

"Do I need to dress for dinner? This seems like the kind of place where I should put a ball gown on just to sit at the table."

"You know, I think Mrs. Brinkley would prefer that, but I'm happy for you to wear jeans and a T-shirt. And you know Daniel won't care. I doubt if he even realizes that you're wearing jeans as it is. He's not one to notice anything any woman wears. Even me."

"Well, that's sad."

Brenda winked. "He notices *some* of the things I wear, of course."

"Of course." Michelle laughed. "Seth notices that kind of thing as well."

"I'm sure he does!"

"So Seth tells me that you have another friend who was matched through Matchrimony, and that's how you heard about it."

Brenda nodded, leading the way out of the room and back down the stairs. "A college friend of mine, Michaela, married a pastor and moved to Oklahoma where he has a congregation."

"That's wonderful."

"She's really happy. Although, from what I heard, their honeymoon did not go according to plan." Brenda related the mishaps of the other couple's honeymoon, setting Michelle off in hysterics again.

"Oh, that's awful. Someone should write a book about that!"

"As long as it's not a romance novel. I don't know how a romance writer could ever delay the sex for that long. Poor Michaela and Jon."

"Sounds like it." Michelle smiled when they entered the dining room and she saw that Daniel and Seth were there waiting for them.

Michelle sat next to Seth and across from Brenda. Seth was across from Daniel. "The room Brenda put us in is beautiful. Thanks for allowing us to stay here," she said to Daniel.

"Happy to have you. Seth is my best friend. I tend to do whatever he wants me to do."

Seth let out a bark of laughter. "You don't expect anyone to believe that, do you?"

Daniel grinned. "Hey, she doesn't know me yet. She might believe it!"

Brenda shook her head. "Daniel doesn't do anything just to please someone else."

The man in question picked up Brenda's hand, kissing it softly. "Except you."

Brenda smiled at him, seeming to get lost in his eyes for a moment. "Except me."

Michelle hoped she and Seth were in love the same way Brenda and Daniel were in a few months, but she knew it was a false hope. No one who wasn't related to her would ever be able to love her unconditionally. She just wasn't the kind of woman people could love.

Seth noticed a sad look cross Michelle's

face, and he took her hand, squeezing it under the table. "Are you okay?"

She nodded. "Of course. I'm just tired from all the travel."

"It has been kind of whirlwind lately. Don't worry. I don't have to go anywhere for three weeks after we get home."

"That will be nice." Honestly she didn't care where they were as long as she could be with him. She sighed. She was already in love with him. How was she going to be able to hide it for the next fifty years or so? She didn't want him to think that he had to tell her he loved her back, simply because she couldn't said she loved him. No, she'd be good and hide it from him.

Chapter Seven

After dinner, Brenda and Michelle went to their respective rooms to change into their swim suits. Once Michelle was wearing her modest one-piece suit, she pulled a swim suit cover up over her head. She hated parading around feeling like she was mostly naked.

The men had gone to Daniel's study to talk business, so the ladies were on their own. Michelle enjoyed being with Brenda so she didn't mind.

The two went out to the pool and swam for a while before sinking into the hot tub. Michelle leaned back in the tub and sighed contentedly. "I needed this."

Brenda nodded. "I find I need it most nights. Makes me happy to relax."

"Seems like the perfect ending to a day to me."

"Tell me about your school. I know you said it's small. I want to know about your students. Do you have favorites?"

Michelle smiled. "Asking me to pick favorites would be like asking a mother to choose her favorite children. I do have a couple of students that I've grown closer to, but all of them are equal in my eyes." She stared up at the stars for a moment before continuing. "There's a group of students, and I've yet to figure out who they are, who wash my car at least once per month. The football team has put together a rotation to mow my lawn, and they won't let me pay them. There are so many things the kids do for me when I'm not expecting it."

"Oh, that's so sweet!"

"Of course, I go above and beyond for

them as well, and I'm sure that's why they do it." Michelle briefly explained about the girls' track team she coached. "I ran in college, but just for fitness. I was pudgy when I started my freshman year, and I didn't like it, so I took up running. I never joined a team or anything, I just ran early in the morning before I went to class."

"I run if there are bears chasing me," Brenda said very seriously.

"There are bears in this area?" Michelle asked surprised.

"Nope. And that's why I don't ever run."

Michelle laughed. "Well, I run. I still run most mornings during the school year, but I run with my track team as well. I go to every single sporting event. That's four nights a week, nine months out of the year. The school district insists that Wednesday nights are kept free for religious activities."

"I like that rule!"

"I do too, because it gives me a break! I use Wednesday nights to catch up on the sleep I miss the rest of the week."

"So why did you talk to Dr. Lachele? When my friend Michaela told me what she'd done, I thought she was nuts, but then I found myself doing the same thing a few months later."

Michelle frowned, not sure how much of the story Seth would want his friends to know. She wasn't going to lie though. "I was engaged for almost three years. A couple of months ago, my fiancé asked me to meet him for dinner on a Wednesday night. I tried to talk him out of it, but he said it was urgent." She sighed. "He wanted to tell me his mistress was pregnant. He had to marry her to give the baby a name, but he was willing to divorce her once the baby was born so he could marry me."

"He did *not* say that to you!" Brenda's voice was filled with shock.

"Oh, he did. I told him I wanted nothing to do with him." Michelle shook her head. "The worst part of it was that I was in a restaurant in my town where everyone knows me. I couldn't even throw my drink in his face, or stand up and start screaming at him. I had to sit there calmly like I wasn't angry."

"That's wrong!"

"I called Dr. Lachele the next day. I didn't see a need to lose all the time and money I'd put into my wedding and reception. Or the honeymoon. So I called Dr. Lachele, and she came and did her tests. My stipulation was that I wanted the wedding on the same day I was supposed to marry Bob."

Brenda shook her head at that. "Please tell me Seth knows about that. If he doesn't, you have to tell him right away. He'll be so angry if he finds out you hid it from him."

Michelle sighed. "He found out when I had to give my first name and Bob's last name for my reservations at Disney."

"No way!"

"Oh, yeah. And you're right. He wasn't happy. We talked through it, though, and we're good now. He's pretty stubborn and opinionated, but we were able to finally find common ground there."

"Wow. I'm surprised he's speaking to you even now. He must really want your marriage to work."

"We both do. He's a good man."

"Oh, he is, but he's not the most forgiving man I've ever met. I heard that he dated the same girl all through college, and she broke it off to go to Hollywood to be an actress. Daniel said she called him every day for a year to try to get him to forgive her, but he just kept telling her that she'd made her choice. She wanted a career more than she wanted him. So she needed to keep her career."

"I heard about the girl, but not about her calling after she got there. Wow. I had no clue."

"Yeah, so I'm impressed he's forgiven you. He doesn't easily."

Michelle frowned. "I doubt if he would have forgiven so easily if we hadn't already been married. He made us sleep with the Berlin Wall between us on our honeymoon."

"The Berlin Wall? At Disney?"

"We made a wall out of pillows in the middle of the bed, and we kept calling it the Berlin wall. I know, it was silly, but it felt unsurmountable for a while."

"That sounds just like Seth. I'm glad you

two got past it. I'm not going to ask how, because I have a feeling I don't want to know."

Michelle's cheeks flamed. She was glad it was too dark to be seen. "You probably don't."

"You were right," Seth said loudly from the direction of the house. "They gave up on swimming and are sitting in the hot tub."

"Yup. I know my wife." Daniel climbed into the tub beside Brenda.

The men had taken time to change into their swim trunks before joining them. Seth climbed in and slid an arm around Michelle's shoulders. "Are you having fun?"

Michelle nodded. "I really am. Brenda is a lot of fun to be around."

"I'm glad. I'll be gone from seven to seven tomorrow to work on Daniel's system, and then Thursday I'll work for my other client.

Friday we'll head out to see my mom. You're going to need someone to entertain you."

"Is she expecting us?" Michelle wanted to put off meeting his mother. She was surprised at how scared she was about meeting the other woman. What if her new mother-in-law hated her?

"She is. You don't need to worry, though. She'll love you."

"Where is your brother? You said you had a twin brother, right?"

"Yeah, I do. Slade is in Dallas-Fort Worth. He's a doctor."

"Doesn't it bother her that you moved to Louisiana then?"

He shook his head. "Her brothers and sisters all live close. She's a nurse and has worked at the same hospital in Boston for twenty-two years. No, it doesn't bother her at all. We haven't had a lot of time to spend together since I went off to college anyway."

"Well, I'm glad to hear she won't resent me for that."

Seth laughed at the idea. "Daniel, tell Michelle my mother has never held a grudge in her life!"

Daniel shook his head. "From what I can see, the woman is perfect. How she ended up with a head-strong opinionated idiot like Seth for a kid, I'll never know. He doesn't deserve her."

Michelle hid a laugh by coughing. "I don't know if I can live up to that kind of perfection."

Seth shrugged. "She's going to love you just because you're my wife. No one else can give her grandbabies."

"Does she want grandbabies?"

"No idea. She's been on us to marry, though, so I think she does. She believes you should only nag about one thing at a time, so she's been nagging me about marrying, not about babies. I'm sure we'll find out when we see her, because she'll move onto the next thing to nag about."

"Why wasn't she wasn't at the wedding?"

He shook his head. "I told her too late, and she realized she wouldn't have any time to spend with me if she came. So she stayed home and told me I needed to bring you to meet her as soon as I could."

"I'm not going to get out of meeting her this trip, am I?"

"Nothing short of a hospitalization would keep me from taking you to her. And if you were hospitalized, I'd just make sure you ended up in the hospital she works at, and you'd meet her there instead."

Michelle looked at Brenda who was watching them closely. "I have a feeling I'm not going to get out of going to meet her."

"I told you he's pig-headed. He's decided you're meeting and nothing is going to stop it from happening."

Seth looked at Brenda, raising one eyebrow. "You told my wife I'm pig-headed?"

"Sure. Someone has to list your flaws. Sometimes you seem a bit too perfect."

Seth shook his head. "I'm not sure I want you two hanging around together after all."

"That's too bad," Michelle told him, "because we're going to shop tomorrow, and she's taking me to Plymouth. I get to see the rock!"

"It's smaller than you think it is," Seth told her.

"I don't have any expectations at all, so I'm sure it will be just fine."

"Don't buy too much garbage."

"I need new school clothes for this year,"

she told him. "It's either shop here with a friend, or drive into New Orleans to get something decent when I get home."

"Why do you need new?"

Michelle shrugged. "I've been wearing the clothes I made for myself when I graduated from college for years. I have a savings account for this type of thing, and the clothes are getting threadbare. It's time for new."

"I didn't know you could sew," he said with surprise.

"You've only known me for a week. There are lots of things you don't know yet."

"There are things you don't know about me as well."

"I know you're pig-headed. What else is there?"

Seth looked over at Daniel, whose face was lit up with amusement. "Do you see what I put up with? If she's like this after a week, how's she going to be acting in a year?"

"Quit bragging. I see you found the right girl for you. No need to rub it in. I found the perfect girl for me, too. And I found mine first!"

Seth laughed, looking down at Michelle. "If only she weren't so tiny. I feel like she'd fit in my pocket."

"Imagine if you'd really gotten a girl just like Brenda. You'd never be able to find her in a crowd, because she's so darn short."

Brenda folded her arms over her chest. "Let's not bring Brenda into this. I'm the perfect size for a Brenda, and that's what really matters."

"Whatever you say," Daniel said, obviously placating her.

"Don't you start with me, Daniel Axford! I'm not afraid to kick you!"

Daniel looked over at Seth. "Someday

she'll realize that being kicked with teeny tiny little feet really doesn't hurt. Until then, I'll act like it's a real threat."

Seth laughed, shaking his head. "You two are a mess. How do you manage to get along without me here to run interference?"

"We get along just fine, thank you very much!" Daniel put his arm around Brenda's shoulders, not moving an inch, even when she pushed him with all her strength.

"I think I'm going to have to be mad at you for a while," Brenda told her husband.

"You do that. Let me know when you're done being mad, so I know when it's safe." Daniel rolled his eyes as he said it.

Brenda looked at her husband. "And you know it's not safe, because I'm tiny but fierce, right? And don't you dare call me a hobbit, or I *will* kick you!"

"Sure. That's exactly what I meant."

Brenda glared at him, but she didn't say anything else, leading Michelle to believe that Daniel had a fight coming later.

Michelle yawned, resting her head sleepily on Seth's shoulder. "All this travel really is getting to me. I'm not a night person anyway."

Seth wrapped his arm around her, holding her against him. "Maybe we should head to bed."

Michelle shook her head. "I'm not going to be a party pooper. You stay down here. I'll go on up."

"Not a chance. I have to be up early, and I'm not much of a morning person. I need to hit the hay or the boss-man will yell at me tomorrow."

Michelle looked at Daniel. "Do you yell?" He didn't seem like the type to have to raise his voice. He was just a natural leader.

"Rarely. I don't have to. I keep my voice quiet, and they all know it's time to run for cover."

Brenda nodded emphatically. "He has the meanest whisper you've ever heard!"

Daniel didn't respond to his wife's comment. He obviously found her ridiculous.

Michelle stood up from the water, patting herself dry with the towel Brenda had given her before coming outside. Seth got out as well. "I'll see you in the morning. I assume you're going in with me at seven."

Daniel nodded. "Of course. I wouldn't let you take my car. I've seen you drive."

"You have four cars. You could loan me one of the others."

"I repeat. I've *seen* you drive."

Seth looked at Michelle. "I don't know why we've been friends for so long. You'd think I'd have buried his body at sea by now, wouldn't you?"

Michelle refused to get into that. "G'night," she called to Brenda and Daniel as she headed for the house.

"You could have defended me there," Seth said as he opened the back door for her.

"I could have..."

"You're as bad as they are!" he complained. "I thought you were on my side. You *are* my wife, you know."

"I'm fully aware."

Seth sighed. "Why is it that I feel abused by everyone around me?"

"You must have a victim complex," Michelle informed him, refusing to play his games.

When they got up to the room, she showered, not wanting to sleep with chlorine on her skin, because often it made her break out when it wasn't washed off immediately.

When she was dressed for bed, she walked back into the room to find Seth reading a book in a chair beside the bed. She'd never really been able to read sitting up, preferring to plop down on a bed on her stomach to read. "Your mystery?"

He nodded. "I think I know who dunnit."

"I'm sure you do."

"Is that meant to be sarcastic? I think Daniel's rubbing off on you."

"No, it's not meant to be sarcastic, and Daniel hasn't rubbed me even once." She slipped between the sheets, yawning widely. "Are you going to shower before bed?"

He nodded. "Yeah. I need to." He put his book down and disappeared into the bathroom. When he came back out ten minutes later, she was curled on her side with one hand tucked under her cheek, sound asleep. He sighed. She really was exhausted.

*****

Brenda and Michelle had a long leisurely breakfast after the men had gone off to work the following morning. "Why didn't the men eat with us?" Michelle asked.

"They were in a hurry. They're always in a hurry." Brenda rolled her eyes. "They do this thing called working for a living. I don't know why..."

Michelle grinned. "I guess I'm the same way during the school year." She'd slept 'til six that morning and was quite proud of herself until she remembered she was on East Coast Time. It was the same as getting up at five at home.

"The stores open up at ten, but if we want to do the ocean walk in Plymouth, I think we should do that first. I don't want it to get hot and crowded before we get there."

"You know better than I do. I'll do

whatever."

"Okay, well, wear something comfortable. Shorts and a tank top are fine. We'll hit the ocean walk, and then go back into Boston for shopping. What kind of clothes do you want to get for school? That'll give me some idea of where to take you."

Michelle thought about it for a moment. She'd always worn business suits to work, but she really didn't need to. None of the other principals in the district did. It's just what she had. She liked the idea of dressing a bit more femininely. "I guess business casual is fine. Maybe some slacks and some nice tops. A couple of skirts." She'd worn high heels to work every day for the past four years. It would be so nice to be able to wear flats.

"Works for me. I have a couple of places in mind. We'll have fun picking stuff out for you."

Thirty minutes later, they were on their way out the door. Brenda had a small car, which was great for navigating the busy Boston traffic. They chatted while they drove. Brenda told some silly stories about her two sisters who both had names similar to hers. "No one could ever remember our names at all. The teachers at school were forever calling me by my older sister's name. Don't name your kids cutesy names like Brenda, Brianna and Brooke. They won't love you for it!"

Michelle laughed. "I don't plan on it. I don't have names picked out yet, of course, but I promise not to play the cutesy game."

Plymouth was fun for Michelle. She'd grown up close to the ocean, and close to New Orleans, a place of historical significance, but it had nothing on the town where the Mayflower touched down. They strolled through the shops, trying on silly hats, and looking at little mementos of the Pilgrims.

"I think I need to get a lobster hat," Michelle announced.

"How could you come to Massachusetts and not buy a lobster hat?" Brenda asked, her face perfectly serious.

"I really don't know. I couldn't even try. It would be sacrilegious, wouldn't it?"

"Definitely. That one looks great on you." Brenda dug through a bin of silly hats. "I think you should get this turkey hat for Seth. He'd thank you for it."

"Wouldn't it be fun for us to wear these to some of the games my school plays in? Then the kids could search for the hats, and not our faces. They get so excited when they see me there."

"That could really be fun." Brenda grinned at Michelle.

"Oh, for the first game he goes to with me, we'll have to wear our bride and groom mouse ears from Disney."

"Seth didn't really wear those, did he?"

"He did! He looked so adorable." Michelle fished her phone out of her purse and quickly flipped through the pictures. "Here, look. We took a selfie with them on." She handed Brenda her camera so she could see the picture they'd taken in front of Cinderella's Castle with the mouse ears on.

Brenda laughed. "You have got to text that to me. Daniel would get a huge kick out of it."

"Sure. What's your number?"

Brenda rattled off her number, and Michelle sent the text. "Now we have each other's numbers. I can text you when I get home."

"Sounds good. I really don't want to lose

touch."

"We won't. I promise." Michelle linked her arm through Brenda's after paying for the silly hats. It was the last shop in Plymouth they wanted to see. "Now what?"

"Now on to the serious shopping. Let's go get you some clothes for school this year." Brenda grinned. "I bet all the boys in your school have a crush on the principal."

Michelle looked at her with shock. "No they don't! You're joking, right?"

Brenda gaped at her friend. "Do you not have any inkling what you look like? They do have mirrors in Louisiana, right?"

"Of course, but I'm just me."

"I had a friend when I was in college that was overweight in high school, and she lost weight the summer before we started college. For the first three years of college, she never had a date, because when guys asked her out she either thought they were making fun of her or pitying her, because she still thought of herself as the overweight teenager she'd been. We finally convinced her that she was pretty, and boys were asking her out because they liked what they saw, but it took forever."

"That's not what's happening with me," Michelle protested. "I dated the same man for nine years!"

"But did you think he just dated you because he felt sorry for you?"

"I—of course not. I don't know why he dated me. It's not like he was faithful anyway."

"Michelle, you're a beautiful woman. Seth is lucky to have you in his life. I hope you know that."

Michelle just shrugged, hoping Brenda would drop the subject. She got into the car and put her bag in the back. "How long will it take us to get to the shops in Boston?"

Brenda looked at her skeptically for a moment, but then she shrugged. "Not long. There's this great little Italian place I want to go to for lunch. Are you game?"

Chapter Eight

Michelle had a wonderful day with Brenda, the two of them trying on outfits together and having lunch at the Italian place Brenda had suggested. The Italian food made Michelle's taste buds stand up and do flips, and she knew she'd want to go there every time she was in town, which she now hoped would be quite often. It seemed that every time she made a wonderful new friend, it was someone who lived too far for regular lunches and fun shopping days.

After they arrived back at the house, Michelle lugged her bags up the stairs, having a hard time believing she'd purchased seven bags of new clothing for school. Her students were never going to recognize her. She wasn't sure yet if that was a good thing or a bad thing, but she was sure Seth would approve of the new clothes. She'd been a lot more daring with colors and hadn't stuck to the grey and black suits she usually wore to school.

She met up with Brenda a short while later, walking through the garden together. "I can't believe how sore shopping all day made me," Michelle complained. "As much as I run, it's not fair that I could get sore from walking through stores."

Brenda laughed. "It's amazing, isn't it? I do better swimming all day than I do shopping."

"Very crazy." Michelle shook her head. "Are we eating later tonight? Because of the men working late?"

"Yeah. Mrs. Brinkley is going to serve supper at seven-thirty instead of six-thirty. She would never dream of inconveniencing

Daniel."

Michelle grinned at that. "She does seem rather devoted to him."

"That's putting it very mildly. She thinks he walks on water." Brenda shook her head. "Makes me crazy sometimes. I always wonder if she likes me at all or just puts up with me because we're married. Of course, now that I'm pregnant, she's catering to my cravings a bit. I'm sure that's because I'm carrying the prince of her universe."

"Pregnant? Really?"

Brenda laughed, patting her stomach which was still perfectly flat. "Really. I found out the day after we got back from your wedding. I'm still having a hard time believing it myself."

"Do you want a boy or a girl?"

Brenda shrugged. "I'm not terribly picky, but Daniel really wants a boy first. He's determined that he'll need help to protect a daughter's honor."

"Men are really strange. You know that, don't you?"

"They are. I think our two are a little stranger than most." Brenda sighed.

"Well, they're both nerds. I think that makes them a little weirder automatically. Sweeter, but weirder too." Michelle looked at her friend. "I'm happy for you."

"Do you and Seth want kids?" Brenda asked.

Michelle nodded. "And I'm thirty-two. I want them right off, because I know I want more than one. I know it's harder to get pregnant as you get older."

"I'm sure that will make Seth very happy."

"Yeah, I think so. He keeps telling me he's happy to help me make them."

Brenda laughed. "Sounds like something Daniel would say. I can see why those two are such good friends."

"I'm surprised Seth doesn't just work for Daniel full time. Seth said he was Daniel's first employee."

"Yeah, Daniel wants Seth to work for him full time, but Seth won't go for it. He likes having his freedom."

"I guess I can't complain, because he wouldn't have been as willing to move to Louisiana if he hadn't had his own business." Michelle couldn't imagine living anywhere but Louisiana. She enjoyed visiting other places, but Malloy was her home.

"Very true. Have you given any thought to moving here? I'm sure there's a school you could work for."

Michelle shook her head. "I couldn't leave the kids. I love Malloy, and I've lived there my whole life. No, that was one of my stipulations when I went to Dr. Lachele. I needed a man who was willing to move to Louisiana to be near me."

"I guess you'll just have to visit. Often."

"And you two are welcome to visit us anytime. I have a spare room. It's nothing like the Rose Room, of course…"

"Well, nothing is…"

Both dissolved into peals of laughter. "I'm so glad you haven't had time to get all rich and snobbish and are willing to talk to the little people like me," Michelle said with a grin.

Brenda wrinkled her nose. "Can you see me doing that? I'd gouge out my own eyes first. I don't have that kind of personality at all."

"I know. And that's the reason I can tease you about it." Michelle smiled. "So will you raise your baby yourself, or will you have a nanny do it?"

Brenda laughed out loud at that, a tinkling laughter that filled the garden. "I'm sure I'll do most of the work myself. I may hire someone to help on occasion so I can leave and do things I want to do."

"Like your volunteer work?"

"Oh, for starters. I don't see myself leaving the baby often though. I'm planning to breast feed, and babies tend to eat pretty often."

"I've heard that..."

Brenda grinned. "I'm glad we're friends. I was kind of worried when I saw you at the church on your wedding day that you'd be snooty. Most pretty girls are."

"And that's why I'm not." Michelle couldn't figure out why Brenda kept referring to her as pretty. She understood why Seth did, and knew for him it must be motivated by a desire for sex. Brenda got nothing out of it though.

"You really need to look in a mirror, girl! You're gorgeous. Everyone thinks so."

"How do you know what everyone thinks?"

"Well, Daniel, Seth, and I think so. Who else matters?"

Michelle laughed. "No one, apparently. You three make up the *entire world*."

"Of course we do!" Brenda stopped at a wooden swing in the very back of the garden and sat down, patting the spot beside her.

Michelle tried to keep a straight face as she realized Brenda's legs didn't reach all the way to the ground, so she sat down and started the swing in motion with one foot. "The gardens are beautiful."

"I think so. It's a wonderful place to live."

"I can see that. The only thing missing is a body of water back here."

"The pool is good enough for me," Brenda responded, a far-away grin on her face. "And we're sure not far from the nearest ocean. Daniel and I go to the beach often."

"You do? He seems like such a workaholic. I have a hard time imagining him taking a day off to go."

Brenda frowned. "We had that problem early in our marriage, but I managed to convince him that taking me to the beach was just as important as working."

"How'd you do that?"

Brenda shrugged. "I made it clear that if he wanted a marriage, I was happy to have one. If he wanted someone who was just going to be there for sex and have babies, then he'd have to find someone else."

Michelle grinned. "I'm impressed. He

doesn't seem to be easily swayed."

"Oh, he's not. But he does enjoy sex, and there's only one place he can get it from."

"That's very true. Unless he wants to pay a whole lot of alimony, that is."

"He doesn't." Brenda smiled. "He loves his business, and he has built it from the ground up. I've never seen anyone who works as hard as Daniel. I'm going to convince him to take time off on occasion to come see you guys now."

"It'd probably be easier if we came here to see you. How long is it safe for you to travel?"

"Oh, I can fly up until the third trimester. I'm healthy. There are no problems with the pregnancy." Every time Brenda mentioned her pregnancy or the baby she carried, she put a hand to her stomach. Michelle thought the action was adorable.

"Glad to hear it." Michelle rested her head on the back of the swing, enjoy the sunshine on her face. She wasn't much of a sun person, but Massachusetts was a break from the hotter sun of Louisiana. It felt like early spring, not almost summer.

Brenda glanced at the display on her phone. "We need to get back to the house. It's supper time."

Michelle nodded, standing up. "I can't believe how tired I am. I may need to go to bed at eight tonight."

Brenda threaded her arm through Michelle's. "No one would be offended if you did."

"What are we doing tomorrow?" Michelle asked as they walked toward the house together.

"Tomorrow is my day to hold babies in the NICU. The hospital always needs extra people. Do you want to join me?"

Michelle smiled, loving the idea. "Yeah, that sounds awesome. I'd love to."

As they walked, Brenda explained how it worked. "The babies they give us are usually babies of mothers addicted to drugs, so they've been abandoned. Occasionally, we'll be given a baby whose mother finds it a hardship to drive into town every day. They all just need love. I tend to sing to them and hold them."

"I can do that." Michelle was surprised at how much she looked forward to it. She'd always loved children, but special education had never been her calling.

"Good. The hospital will be happy with an extra volunteer, even if it's only for one day."

When they got to the house, Daniel and Seth were just sitting down at the table. "We were getting worried about you two," Seth said, getting back to his feet.

Michelle walked to him, kissing him softly. It was the first day they'd spent apart since they'd married. "Did you have a good day?"

"Mostly. I got what I needed to do done without the boss-man yelling too much."

She sat down beside him, taking his hand in hers. "I'm glad you didn't get yelled at."

"Did you get the shopping you needed to do done?" he asked.

"And then some. Brenda took me to some really nice shops, and I got some good deals." She'd shopped mostly clearance, but she didn't tell him that. She didn't want him to think she needed him to give her money for clothes when she had enough to make it through. Besides, he was going to be doing a lot more travelling for business, and she refused to be a leach on his income.

"Good! So you won't need to shop as soon as we get back to Louisiana."

She shook her head. "No, I won't. I have enough clothes to make it through the schoolyear with no problem." Unless she got pregnant, of course, but they'd deal with that when they had to.

Seth looked over at Daniel. "So do I get to borrow a car tomorrow and Friday? Or should I go rent one?"

Daniel seemed to think hard about the answer. "I guess. Just be careful."

Seth rolled his eyes. "I'll be careful. Wreck one car and the man never forgets it."

"You wrecked a car with me in it!"

"But it wasn't even my fault! Someone pulled out in front of me!"

"So? You wrecked the car. I thought I was going to die." Daniel laid the back of his hand against his forehead dramatically.

"You didn't even get a scratch!" Seth shook his head at his friend. "Why do I even talk to you?"

"Glutton for punishment?"

Michelle and Brenda laughed at the two of them. "I'm not sure why we put up with either of them," Michelle said to Brenda.

"I dunno. I put up with Daniel, because he's the father of my unborn child. Unless I really was abducted by aliens, and if I was, I'm not admitting it."

Seth grinned. "Pregnant? That's awesome!"

Brenda smiled, her face lit up. "I'm surprised Daniel didn't tell you."

"You told me I couldn't tell anyone until you told your mother." Daniel frowned at her.

"I called her a week ago."

"Why didn't you tell me that?" Daniel asked, looking disgusted.

Brenda shrugged. "You didn't ask." She paused for a moment, before turning to Daniel fully, putting her fork down. "Hey Daniel?"

"Yeah?"

"I told my parents about the baby, and you're now free to tell anyone you want."

"I'm taking out a skywriter."

"Be my guest." Brenda resumed eating, acting for all the world like taking a skywriter out to announce a pregnancy was normal.

Seth looked at Michelle. "When you get pregnant I won't take out a skywriter. I promise. I think that's tacky."

Michelle shrugged. "Well, of course it is. But Daniel doesn't seem to do anything halfway. I think he secretly likes tacky."

"I know he does." Seth shook his head. "In college, he had fuzzy dice hanging from his rearview mirror. You'd have thought it was the seventies."

"So sad." Michelle shook her head.

Brenda gave Daniel a pitying look. "I'm so glad your taste is better now. And we all know it is, because you married me."

Daniel made a face. "Yeah, but someone else chose you for me. Wait 'til you see the clothes I'm buying for the baby."

"Just don't buy him any red shirt Star Trek uniforms. He doesn't need to die!"

Daniel frowned. "I'll try. It's hard, though, because the red shirts say the funniest stuff!"

"My child will not be your walking talking nerd billboard. Do you hear me, Daniel?"

Michelle bit her lip to stifle a laugh, and looked at Seth, who was watching her. "Whatever she says to Daniel about dressing babies goes double for you, Seth Henderson."

Daniel looked at Michelle. "You're not

already pregnant, are you?"

Michelle blushed beet red. "No, I'm not. I'm just getting it out of the way for the future."

"Fine, fine, fine." Seth frowned at her. "You know I have impeccable taste in clothes. Look at the hat I wore all around Disney."

Daniel looked back and forth between Seth and Michelle. "Wait. Hat? I need to see this hat. Or photographic evidence thereof."

Brenda fished out her phone and showed him the text Michelle had sent her earlier that day. "Don't they both look adorable?"

Daniel's grinned spread over his entire face. "Henderson, you've got it bad. You posed in front of a Disney castle wearing those ridiculous mouse ears? Why not just let her put a leash around your joystick and lead you around that way?"

Michelle let out a gasp of surprise before

laughing. "Joystick?"

Seth smiled at Michelle, his lips going to her ear. "I hope Mr. Happy brings you plenty of joy."

Michelle shook her head, refusing to join in the conversation. "I think we need to change the subject. Quickly." She wracked her brain for something to change it to. She was not going to calmly discuss penises at the dinner table. "I got you a hat while we were in Plymouth today."

Seth frowned. "A hat?"

"Yes, but nothing like the hat I got you at Disney. I figure you can wear it to the games we go to."

"I'm intrigued and frightened all at once. Will I like this hat?"

"Oh, of course you will! I wouldn't buy you anything you wouldn't like." Michelle took another bite of her grilled vegetables, a big smile on her face. "You're going to adore it."

Seth looked at Daniel, his eyes round. "Why do I get the feeling I'm going to regret letting her shop with your wife?"

Daniel shrugged, digging into his own food. "Because you're not *quite* as stupid as you look?"

Michelle looked at Brenda. "Let's never talk to each other the way they do. They sound like they're high schoolers trading insults."

Brenda nodded. "Dorky high schoolers at that!"

After dinner, the two men went back to Daniel's office again. "What do they do back there? They can't be talking business all that time!" Michelle shook her head in disbelief.

"Oh, they're not. They're playing video games. I guarantee it."

"Daniel has a video game console in his office?"

"It's the only way he can sneak and play and make me think he's working. He doesn't know I know about it, but I do."

"When are you going to call him on it?" Michelle asked, a sparkle in her eye.

"Oh, I'll wait until the time is just right, and then I'll say something. He won't know what hit him."

Michelle smiled. "I do like the way you think."

"Let's go for a swim. They'll join us, I'm sure."

That night, Michelle was happy to just hang out in the pool. She and Brenda swam laps for a while, before they sat on the sides of the pool with their feet dangling in the warm water. "I enjoy your pool and hot tub."

"You should. They're awesome."

"I just have a swamp, and I can't swim in it because alligators."

"Yeah, alligators scare me even more than bears."

"Maybe if you swam in the swamp, you'd feel the need to run a bit more than you do."

Brenda shook her head. "Nah. I like not running. I swim for my exercise."

"More fun and cooler," Michelle said with a nod. "I approve."

"Your approval is all that matters to me."

They heard laughter as the men headed out to join them. Daniel made a clean dive into the pool, and as soon as he did, Seth did a cannonball, landing right in front of him.

"So rude!" Daniel said when he came up sputtering.

Brenda and Michelle watched the men as they frolicked in the water, pushing and splashing each other as if their lives depended on it. "They act like little boys. Are they always this way?" Michelle asked.

"No. Seth is a lot more relaxed since you guys got married. I think he needed to find the right woman for him."

Michelle frowned at that. She didn't know if she was the right woman for anyone. She knew no one would ever love her, so she worried that Seth would realize it and hate her eventually. She hoped not, but how could he not realize how unlovable she was eventually?

"Should we join them?" Brenda asked after a long pause.

Michelle shook her head. "I'm not getting in the middle of that nonsense. What if they turn on me?"

Brenda laughed. "You make a good point, my friend. I have an unborn child to protect." She put her hands down over her belly as if protecting the child.

Daniel stopped messing around and rushed to Brenda's side. "Are you okay? Is something wrong with the baby? What's happening?"

Brenda laughed. "The baby is fine, and so is his mama. Go back to acting like a child."

"Why did you grab your stomach then? Are you sure the baby's okay?" The sheer panic in Daniel's voice brought tears to Michelle's eyes. Someday she hoped someone would be able to love her that way. She wasn't holding her breath though.

"I was just playing around. I told Michelle I couldn't get in the water with you two because you might hurt the baby."

Daniel's eyes grew wide. "I'll stop messing around. I promise. We won't hurt the baby. You can swim."

Brenda laughed. "That's not what I'm saying. We already swam. I'm good. I was just making a joke. I won't do that again."

Daniel frowned. "Are you sure?"

"I'm absolutely positive. Go play with your friend." After he'd gone back to swim some more, Brenda looked at Michelle and rolled her eyes. "Sometimes, it's hard to believe that anyone can love me that much. But he does."

Michelle sighed. "I want that someday. I envy you a great deal. And it's not for your pool, hot tub, or huge house. I don't even envy you Daniel. I envy the way he loves you. I need that in my life."

Brenda smiled, putting her hand on Michelle's arm. "You get the same from Seth. You just don't see it yet. I promise you, he feels the same way about you that Daniel does about me."

Michelle shook her head, feeling a tear prick her eye. She wished her friend was right with everything inside her, but she knew better.

Chapter Nine

On Friday morning, Seth drove Michelle to his mother's apartment in Boston. It was in a quiet little community. "She's lived here for about fifteen years," he told Michelle as they climbed the stairs to the second story apartment.

Michelle gripped his hand tightly while he knocked on the door, more nervous than she'd been walking down the aisle toward Seth. She took breaths slowly in through her nose and out through her mouth, trying to calm herself. She had no idea what to expect, and that made it so much harder for her.

When the door was opened, Michelle stared at the tall, smiling woman on the other side. "Seth!" Mrs. Henderson grabbed her son in a hug, holding him against her, before she turned her attention to Michelle. "And you must be Michelle."

"It's nice to meet you, Mrs. Henderson."

"Oh, call me Judy. Mrs. Henderson was *my* mother-in-law." She opened the door wider, inviting them both inside. "I'm so happy to finally meet you. I'm sorry I couldn't make it down for the wedding, but it would have been hard to get someone to cover my shift at the last minute."

"Seth told me you're a nurse."

Judy nodded. "I'm an oncology nurse at a local hospital. I get to know my patients, because they tend to be in and out of the hospital."

"It must be hard when you lose them." Michelle had lost one student to a car accident in her first year as principal, and she could still feel the grief that had surrounded the entire school. She wasn't sure if it was worse to lose someone to a long, slow death or one that was completely unexpected.

"It is. Harder than I can describe. But each one leaves something of himself behind. I wouldn't trade jobs for anything in the world." Judy waved Seth and Michelle toward the couch. "Sit down. What do you do, Michelle?"

"I'm a high school principal in a tiny little town in Louisiana."

"I've never been to Louisiana. Do you like it there?"

Michelle shrugged. "It's all I've ever known. I love my students, and my little school. I have a great family that I live very close to. It's a wonderful place." She was fully aware of the flaws of her state, and especially of the education system, but she couldn't imagine living anywhere else.

"Is it really as wild as people read about during Mardi Gras?"

"Yes. I've never actually been to New Orleans for Mardi Gras, though. My little town has its own parade, on a much smaller and less debauched scale, and I attend every year. Usually it's a couple of my students serving as king and queen of the parade."

"Maybe I'll try to come down for your little town's parade this year. Would that be all right?" Judy asked Michelle.

"Oh, yes, ma'am. Of course it would! We have a spare room you could use. I'd love to get to know you better."

Judy laughed. "I'm a mother-in-law. Of course you don't want to know me better."

Michelle smiled at that. "But I do. I look forward to you visiting."

Seth looked at Michelle. "You said that without looking like you wanted to throw up.

I'm really impressed."

Judy looked at her son. "Behave yourself. I remember meeting my mother-in-law for the first time, and your sarcasm will only make things worse." She hovered in the doorway. "Can I get you something to drink? Iced tea? Water? Milk? Pepsi?"

Michelle smiled. "I'd love some iced tea if you don't mind."

"I only have sweet. Is that a problem?"

"That's the only way I like it," Michelle responded with a smile.

"Me too, Mom," Seth said. As soon as his mother left for the kitchen, he took her hand in his. "See, she's not scary at all."

Michelle shook her head. "Not yet."

From the other room, Judy called, "When are you two going to start a family? I'm not getting any younger, and I sure want to be young enough to enjoy my grandbabies."

He looked at Michelle and made a face. "Now we know. That's the new thing she'll nag about," he said in a loud whisper.

Michelle elbowed him in the side. "I'd like children right away," she called back to the kitchen.

"Oh, good. I'd like half a dozen or so grandkids. I wanted that many children, but unfortunately, I was only able to get pregnant the once. At least I got two for the price of one." Judy came back into the room carrying two glasses of iced tea, giving one to each. "Seth, move over to the other chair. I want to sit with Michelle."

Seth gave his mother a wary look. "Why?" He didn't trust her at all.

"Just move." Judy gave him a mom-look that made him get up from his chair. Michelle did her best not to laugh. His mother was one of the tallest women she'd ever met, but still

Seth towered over her by five inches. She loved when grown men were cowed by their mothers. It made her have a great deal of respect for the women.

Seth moved into the chair, watching his mother warily. "Why did I move, Mom?"

Judy pulled a photo album from the coffee table and put it between her and Michelle. "I thought you'd want to look at his awkward adolescent photos and all his naked baby pictures."

Michelle stifled a laugh. "Oh, sure. I'd love to."

She flipped through the album, laughing at pictures of Seth in a basketball uniform and the running commentary Judy gave her. In more than half of the pictures, there was another little boy with him—one who looked nothing like him. In their graduation photo, Slade, the twin, appeared to be at least three inches shorter than Seth.

"Seth was always the center on the basketball team, because he was the tallest boy in school. He couldn't make a basket to save his life, though. He was just good at tipping the ball toward his teammates."

"Really?" Michelle asked, glancing up at Seth, who was spending a great deal of time studying his finger nails. "Why didn't your brother come to the wedding?"

Seth sighed. "He planned to make the eight hour drive down from Texas for the day, but he had a difficult delivery the night before and was sure he'd wreck if he tried to drive. Such is the life when you have a doctor for a brother."

Judy smiled when Michelle turned another page. "You should have seen Seth's girlfriend when he was in high school. She was just awful. She was going through that

Goth thing that so many girls did back then. She wore black lipstick and a black formal gown to prom. I swear she looked like she was going to a funeral. Or already dead. One of those."

Michelle flipped the page again to see the girl Judy had been talking about. Seth had his hair spiked all over his head and wore a nice tuxedo. The girl on his arm was glaring at the camera. "What was her name?"

"No idea," Seth responded. "I barely remember her."

"You dated her for four years!" Judy protested. "You'd come home with black lipstick all over you."

Seth blushed. "I did not. Stop it, Mom."

Michelle tried her best not to laugh. She'd have been mortified if her mother was telling all of her secrets that way, but it was amusing since it was Seth's secrets being shared.

"Let's call her Elvira, mistress of the night."

Seth threw his hands up in the air. He knew when he was outnumbered. "I was hoping you two would get along, but not this well," he said with a frown. He'd never envisioned his mother sharing photos of him this way. She'd never done it with any of his girlfriends, but come to think of it, she'd made it clear she never liked any of them.

Judy laughed, turning the page. "You'll survive."

By the time they left several hours later, Michelle felt as if she knew Judy much better. "I can't wait for you to come and visit us in Louisiana. I'll send you the dates we have off school for Mardi Gras."

"Wait, they give you time off school for Mardi Gras?" Judy asked, obviously surprised.

Michelle grinned. "We get more time for

Mardi Gras than we get for Thanksgiving. A full three days. The Monday, Tuesday, and Wednesday of Fat Tuesday week."

"Why do you have Wednesday off? I would think the festivities would be over on Tuesday."

"Oh, they are. Too many hangovers on Wednesday for anyone to actually work or go to school." Michelle shook her head. It had never made much sense to her either.

Judy blinked a couple of times. "Interesting culture."

"I've always thought so." Michelle hugged her new mother-in-law. "Thanks for being wonderful."

"Oh, you're the keeper of my son and grandbabies. I know better than to make you angry."

Michelle laughed as they left, walking down the stairs beside Seth. "I like your mom."

"She likes you too. A little too much, I fear."

Michelle laughed. "Are you and Slade a lot alike? It's weird knowing there's another of you out there."

He shook his head. "Not really. Slade was a lot more studious than I was, if you can believe that. I got into being a video game nerd, but he excelled at school. I played Mario while he was in the chess club. That kind of thing. We were always close, though. It was so weird when we went off to different colleges. We haven't had much time together since. I still miss him sometimes."

"I'd miss my sister if we lived apart. I've never lived more than a twenty-minute drive from her. Makes me sad just thinking about it."

"It's hard."

Michelle saw she was making him sad and changed the subject. "Are we going straight back to Daniel's?" she asked.

He shook his head. "I thought I'd take you to my favorite restaurant, and then we could go for a walk through Boston. Maybe pick up a couple of cannoli."

"I've had cannoli," she responded. "I don't like them very much."

"That's because you've never had Boston cannoli. I promise you, you're going to adore it."

"All right," she responded with a shrug. She was happy to just spend time with him. She'd enjoyed the trip, and all the time she'd gotten to spend with Brenda had been fun, but really, she wanted more time with Seth. She'd never seen herself as a clingy woman, but she was turning into one. She wanted to spend every waking minute in his company.

He took her to a nice restaurant, and she felt underdressed in her jeans and tank top. "I would have worn one of my new outfits if you'd told me how fancy this place was," she hissed at him. She wanted to hide behind him, but he was dressed no better, wearing a pair of jeans and a T-shirt that featured Donald Duck, calling him the original Angry Bird.

"No one cares what you're wearing," he responded. "This place has the best seafood on the planet. You're going to love it."

After they were seated, she looked over her menu. "I don't even recognize a lot of these things. What do I want to eat?"

"Try the stuffed lobster tail. It's one of my favorites."

She nodded. "That's what I'll have then."

"For a side, go with the risotto. You'll love it."

"Done." She reached out and took his

hand in hers. "I really have enjoyed this trip. Thank you for bringing me with you."

"Could I have forced you to stay at home? I got the impression you were coming whether I liked it or not."

She made a face at him. "That's not true. I have to admit I am used to being in charge now. It's odd to share decisions with someone."

He smiled at that. "I've been working for myself since college. I know exactly what you mean."

"Think we can manage?"

He nodded. "I think we can handle anything if we do it together."

The waiter came to their table then, and they placed their orders. Once he was gone, Michelle brought something up. "I've been thinking, and I want your opinion. If you feel strongly one way or the other, I won't argue on it."

Seth raised an eyebrow. "I rarely like conversations that start that way."

Michelle sighed. "No one does." She looked down at her hands for a moment, trying to get the courage to bring up the topic. "I'm thinking about keeping my maiden name professionally. I'd change it legally, and use it for everything but my work."

He studied her for a moment. "And you think that'll bother me?"

She shrugged. "I don't know if it will or not. It would have made Bob spitting mad."

"So you'd have changed your name for Bob? And not for me?"

She shook her head. "I'm honestly more willing to take your name than I was his."

"That makes no sense at all."

"I'm not sure if I can explain it well. Bob expected me to take his name, and would have been angry if I didn't, so I didn't want to. You, however, aren't anything like him, for which I thank God daily. Because you wouldn't try to force me to take your name, I'm more willing to do it. Does that make sense?"

Seth nodded slowly. "I guess it does." It made woman sense to him, meaning it seemed to be something a woman would come up with, but it didn't follow good logic to him. "I don't care if you change your name professionally. You worked hard to get your degrees, and you got them as Michelle Strempel. I don't need you to change your name to Henderson so people will know you're my wife."

"It really wouldn't bother you?" she asked. "I still haven't decided either way, but I wanted you to at least have some input."

He shrugged. "It's completely your

decision. I could argue for either side, but I won't feel like less of a man if you keep your maiden name."

"Thank you."

"What are you thanking me for?" he asked, slightly confused.

"For not trying to control me or tell me how to do things. For accepting that I have a brain in my head. For treating me as an equal." She could go on for hours. She'd thought the way Bob had treated her was normal, because he was her only real relationship. He'd said that people don't really act the way they did in romance novels, and she needed to get over thinking they would.

"The more you say things like that, the more I want to meet Bob. I want to wrap my hands around his neck."

Michelle laughed. "He's not worth the

effort. Besides, he's married to Angela now, and I'm sure they're having fun picking out a nice nursery." She was so glad it was Angela and not her.

"I'm so glad he was an ass, and you didn't marry him."

She blinked a few times. "I guess that's good?"

"It is. If you'd married him, you never could have married me, and let's face it. We belong together. Dr. Lachele thinks so, and I know so. We really are good together."

"We are. We make a good team."

He nodded. "I'm glad you were the one she picked out for me."

"Really?" She still had a hard time believing anyone would prefer her over another woman. Look at Bob. He'd been engaged to her for years while having sex with someone else. Why hadn't she been special enough to wait for?

"Really. I hope you know that I never would have betrayed you like Bob did. In the same position, if you'd told me you wanted to wait 'til we were married for sex, I would have just made the wedding come sooner."

"I wanted to have a faster wedding, but Bob insisted everything needed to be perfect. He said that doing it quickly would never be good enough, because our wedding needed to be the social event of the year."

"Why?" he asked.

"Because that's what his mother wanted. She was awful. The first time I met her, she told me I'd have to take lessons in the proper managing of a household, and she hoped I planned to give up my little hobby as soon as I married. You know, my little hobby that I went to school for six years for, being a high school principal."

He rolled his eyes. "No wonder you were nervous about meeting my mother. She sounds like a real piece of work. I'd like to wrap my fingers around her throat as well."

"How about Bob's dad? You might as well just kill off the whole family."

"You have a point there! I probably should."

Their food came then, and Michelle looked at the stuffed lobster tail curiously. She had no idea what it really was, but she trusted him. She took a small bite of the delicacy, and sighed in contentment. "That's delicious."

He grinned. "I knew you'd like that." He'd gotten the same thing for himself and forked up a big bite of the cheese risotto. "Mom obviously loves the idea of you being the mother of her grandchildren."

"I have a feeling that your mother would

have loved anyone you brought to her who was willing to give birth to her grandchildren."

He chuckled at that. "You might be right, but she really liked you. I could tell."

"I really liked her too. I feel like I was silly for being so nervous about meeting her. She's an incredible woman."

"She is. She gave up her career when she married my father, but after his death, she had to go back to work. She never once complained when we had to move to a smaller house or she had to work double shifts. She just found a way to make it work. I have a ton of respect for her." He shook his head. "She had to see both Slade and I through high school. It would have been bad enough with one son, but two of us really kept her on her toes."

"It sounds to me like she's earned it."

"She has. More than any other woman I know." He smiled. "What about your mom? I know I met her briefly at the reception, but did she work? Or was she a stay at home mom?"

"She always worked for the school. She was the secretary. She took that job because it meant she had the same holidays that my sister and I did."

"Oh, that's perfect."

Michelle nodded. "It worked out very well for us. There was no daycare necessary, because she started doing it when my younger sister was school age."

"What does your dad do?"

"He's an engineer. Works for the city of Malloy."

"So he was the primary bread-winner?"

"Definitely. Mom's income was extra. She'd put it in savings every month, and we'd take family vacations on it, or that's where money for special outfits or dresses came from. Anything beyond our daily needs came from mom's little savings account. We were really blessed. And we had her home with us every summer, running us wherever we wanted to go."

"What did you do in the summers?"

"When I was in high school? I volunteered at our local library. It gave me an excuse to be around books all the time." She got a far-away look, thinking of those glorious summer days spent with all the books she could possibly dream of reading.

"Did you read romance novels in high school?" he asked, a grin on his face.

She shook her head. "No, when I was in high school, I read all the great works of literature, thinking it made me superior to everyone else. I got addicted to romance novels thanks to one of my college roommates. We still recommend books to each other all the time."

He grinned at that. "It sounds like you made some wonderful friends in college."

"I did. I made good friends in high school as well, but it was different. Most of the girls in my high school, which is the school I'm now principal of, were planning to marry as young as they possibly could. Twenty-three was an old maid. Once I was in college, I met a different kind of girl. Ones who cared more about getting an education and building a career than settling down to have families." She shrugged. "Of course, I always wanted a family as well, but I wanted it in conjunction with a career, not just a family."

"I can understand that. I hope you know I'll never ask you to stop working."

"Good, because I don't see it happening. I

enjoy what I do too much. I would feel like I was abandoning my students."

"I admire your dedication to them." He took another bite of his food. "But to get back to how we started this whole thing. You can work as Miss Strempel or Mrs. Henderson, whichever makes you happy."

She smiled, knowing then she'd take his name. Having the option to keep her own was what was really important to her. "Thank you for being so understanding."

"I married you knowing that we would have little things like that to work out. You were a stranger to me, so I've had an open mind about everything since day one. Well, except maybe about going to a honeymoon you'd planned with another man." He frowned at that. He hated that he'd gotten so angry with her, but it had really thrown him for a loop.

"Are you still upset over that? I thought we'd worked it out."

"We have. It just still feels weird. I understand now that you didn't really have feelings for him, but still, it was a blow to realize you'd planned everything with him in mind. He could have been the man wearing the tuxedo mouse ears and not me!"

"Oh, the horror!" Michelle grinned, but at the same time, it would have been awful if Bob had been her groom and not Seth. She loved the man across from her with every fiber of her being, and it had taken only a couple of weeks for it to happen. She'd dated Bob for almost a decade, and had never felt anything but relief when he left her at the end of a date.

"I think it would have been awful. How would I have looked with another woman in mouse ears hanging on my arm? Terrible, I tell you!"

She giggled. "I can just imagine Elvira wearing the bride mouse ears and holding onto you. I wonder if she would have worn white lipstick instead of black…"

"Elvira?" he asked, a frown on his face. After a moment he understood. "Oh, you mean Tiffani. Yeah, that never would have worked out. She was so depressing."

"I'm sure!" Michelle shook her head, trying to come to grips with the girl in the photos being named Tiffani. The name was entirely too sweet and nice for her.

He shook his head at her. "Nope, God and Dr. Lachele brought the perfect woman into my world, and I'm glad I have her."

"God and Dr. Lachele? Are they working as a team now?"

"Sure looks like it from my standpoint." He took her hand and brought it to his lips.

"Whatever name you go by, you're the woman I want in my life."

Michelle sighed. It was sweet of him to say, but she knew he had to be lying. "Thank you."

Chapter Ten

They flew home Saturday after a tearful goodbye with Daniel and Brenda. The two women couldn't stop the tears as they embraced. "Come see us," Michelle said while Daniel and Seth looked on, shaking their heads.

Brenda sniffed. "We will. Hopefully at least once before school starts."

"We'll come back and see you as well," Michelle told her friend. "I can't meet someone I connect with so well and then never see her again."

"There's always Skype," Seth offered helpfully.

Both women glared at him in unison, saying, "It's not the same!"

At their united words, Brenda and Michelle looked at each other and laughed. "We'll come back soon." Michelle hugged Brenda one last time before they headed into the airport.

As they walked away, Seth said, "I guess I should have seen that coming."

"What?" Michelle asked.

"You and Brenda hitting it off like that."

"Why do you say that?"

"You both have kind hearts. I'm not surprised you became so close so quickly."

"Well, we'll just have to visit often," Michelle insisted. "At least every summer."

"So every summer we need to go to both Disney World and Boston? Our travel budget is going to be outrageous."

"I refuse to worry about that right now."

*****

They attended the church where they'd

been married together the following morning, and Michelle enjoyed introducing Seth to her family and friends. "We've been invited to Sunday lunch at my parents' house," she told him in a whisper. "Do you want to go, or should I make our excuses?"

"Oh, I don't mind," he told her. "Your father probably wants to spend a little time with me to get to know me better. Any man would want to know who was taking his daughter to bed every night."

She wrinkled her nose at him. "I'm sure Daddy thinks I'm still a virgin. We're going to leave it that way."

Seth rolled his eyes. "Whatever."

The lunch went well, with her father and Seth getting along beautifully. Her mother pulled her aside as they were clearing the table. "He's a really good man. I think Bob breaking it off was one of the best things that ever happened to you."

Michelle smiled at that. "I think so too. He's been good for me." What she didn't say is that he'd given her a new confidence that she'd never expected.

When they got back home, Michelle started on the laundry from their trip. She knew that Seth was going to set up his office the following day, and she wanted to be able to help him as much as possible.

After she had the laundry started, she joined him in the living room where he was playing a computer game with his laptop. He put his computer down, and invited her to snuggle beside him. "I think I like being married."

Michelle laughed. "I do too. I wasn't sure that I would be able to get used to a stranger touching me so much, but I kind of like it."

"You like strangers touching you? Should

I be worried?" He frowned at her.

She made a face at him. "Not at all. You're not a stranger now, but you were when we married, and it seemed strange. Now it just feels right." She knew she didn't have to tell him how much she enjoyed his touch. It was obvious daily.

He shrugged. "It feels right because there's love between us now."

She blinked a few times in surprise. How did he know she loved him? "How—how did you know I love you? I never said." She'd tried her hardest to hide it from him, because she hadn't wanted him to feel uncomfortable.

"I wasn't sure of your feelings," he said, a grin on his face. "I was referring to my own."

She pulled away from him at his words, a frown on her face. "What do you mean?"

"I mean that I love you. That's what I was saying. I wasn't trying to tell you that you love me."

She got to her feet, shaking her head. "I know better. Please don't ever lie to me again." She turned toward the front door, needing to be alone for a little while. "I have grocery shopping to do." She plucked her keys off the hook where she always put them upon entering the house and walked out the door, slamming it behind her.

When Seth followed her outside, she reversed quickly and left him there, staring after her. *How dare he pretend he loves me? He has no right!*

Seth stood watching her car drive away, wondering what on earth had just happened. He told his wife that he loved her and she accused him of lying and left? What was wrong with her?

He walked back into the house and to the bedroom he'd chosen for his office, immediately going to work disassembling the bed. He needed to do something physical to work off his anger, and there was nothing more physical than moving furniture around. Maybe by the time she got back, he'd be a little bit less angry, and he could deal with her calmly and rationally. Maybe.

*****

Michelle wanted to throw things. She wanted to have the kind of fit no one had seen from her since she was three and her favorite doll had been decapitated by a mean neighbor boy.

"Miss Strempel! How's married life?" A pretty little blond cheerleader named Lauren bounced over to her in the produce aisle, her mother right behind her.

Michelle smiled sweetly. "It's good. It's Mrs. Henderson now." Even in her anger, she couldn't ignore the use of her maiden name.

She was Seth's wife, and she'd use his name with pride.

"Did you go to Disney for your honeymoon?" Lauren asked.

Michelle nodded, wanting nothing but to get away, but knowing she could never be rude to a student that way. "Yes, I did. Do you want to see a picture of us there?" She took out her phone and flipped through to the selfie of the two of them in their bride and groom mouse ears in front of Cinderella's Castle before handing the girl her phone.

Lauren giggled. "Oh, that's awesome. You look so happy! He must really love you to be willing to wear those mouse ears!"

Michelle smiled. "He's a really good man. I'm a lucky woman." And she realized she believed it. She was very lucky to have been married to such a kind, loving man. So why was she so angry with him?

"He looks like it. Will he be going to games with you from now on?"

"Of course. Not all of them, because he travels for business sometimes, but he'll come when he can. I bought us special hats to wear for the games this year."

Lauren smiled at that, knowing her beloved principal would do something fun. "That sounds amazing." She looked over her shoulder to where her mother was picking out produce. "You've met my mom haven't you?"

Michelle nodded. "Your mom and I were in school together." Lauren's mother had been three years ahead of Michelle in school, and had gotten married within a month of graduation.

"Really? She never mentioned that!" Lauren turned back to her mother, who was approaching them with her shopping cart.

"Why didn't you tell me you and Miss Strempel—I mean Mrs. Henderson—went to school together?"

Lauren's mother frowned. "She was a few years behind me, and we didn't exactly run in the same circles. I forgot we went to school together at all."

"You didn't run in the same circles?" Lauren asked. "What does that even mean?"

Michelle smiled. "Your mom was a cheerleader, and she hung out with the popular kids. I was a nerd and spent all my time in the library." And Lauren's mother had taken great pains to tease and torment Michelle, something that didn't happen nearly as often under her watch, because she knew what to watch for.

"You couldn't have been a nerd, Mrs. Henderson! You're the coolest principal ever!"

"I assure you, I was a nerd." Michelle smiled at the very idea that she hadn't been an outcast as a teenager.

Lauren's mother smiled. "She was a nerd, but your dad and I did go to school with her. It's good to see you, Michelle."

"You too. I need to hurry and finish shopping, so I can get home. Newlyweds and all." Michelle didn't know why, but being able to say she was married made her feel validated. She rushed through the rest of her shopping and headed home. She had a husband to apologize to.

*****

Seth finished taking the bed apart and carried the different pieces into the garage. While he worked, he thought about what had happened with Michelle. When she'd first left, he had been angry, wondering what her problem was, but finally it dawned on him.

She didn't think she was worthy of his love.

It made him sad, and he started to think about some way he could show her he loved her. His first choice would have been waiting for her naked, but Michelle wouldn't have found that romantic at all. No, she needed some sort of grand gesture, and he would have to figure out exactly how to make it happen.

A quick call to Brenda helped a little. "Do you know what Michelle's favorite flower is?" he asked.

He made a second phone call to a local florist, putting his plan into action. It would have to happen the next day, and he'd have to find some way to get her out of the house... He called her mother, knowing that would take care of things.

When Michelle arrived home, he acted as if nothing had happened, having her help him carry the dresser from the bedroom out to the garage after she'd put groceries away. "I think that spare room is going to be perfect for what I need."

"Oh good. I was hoping it would. I don't want you to have to waste money on an office when we have plenty of space right here. And then we still have a spare bedroom for guests." She wasn't sure why he was acting like she hadn't been an idiot a couple of hours before, but she was glad. She didn't want to have to try to explain things to him.

That night, in his arms, she told him she loved him again, hoping he'd say the words back to her, so she could react appropriately. Instead, he made love to her, making her feel loved, even without the words.

Her mother called on Monday morning and asked that she meet her for lunch at the restaurant in town. "Mom, I'm a newlywed. I don't want to leave my husband to have lunch with you."

Seth waved a hand at her from the table where he was eating breakfast. "You go. I need to work all day anyway."

Michelle frowned. "Seth said to go. I'll see you there at noon."

*****

As soon as Michelle left the house, Seth sprang into action. He went to the grocery store and picked up the flowers he'd ordered as well as a few other things he'd need to make his romantic gesture complete.

He was waiting in the living room when he heard her pull up and hurried into the bedroom to wait for her reaction to the surprise.

Michelle opened the front door and found a trail of yellow tulips leading from the entryway of the house, down the long hallway, and into their bedroom. She grinned, following the beautiful flower path.

When she reached her bedroom, she gasped with surprise. There were tulips everywhere, making her smile. And on the bed, spelled out in Hershey's miniatures, was, "I love you, Michelle!"

She grinned, looking around for Seth. When she spotted him, leaning against the wall with his arms folded across his chest, she circled the bed and went to him, leaning forward so her cheek was against his chest. "I love you so much."

Seth smiled, his arms going around her. "I love you too. You believe me now, don't you?"

She nodded. "I realized I was an idiot for getting so upset with you yesterday, but when you didn't mention it, I decided to let it go."

"What made you realize that I wasn't

lying to you?" he asked, truly curious about her change of heart. Not that he wasn't thrilled she'd had one. He was simply surprised.

"I ran into one of my students in the produce section, and she asked if we went to Disney World for our honeymoon. I may have a reputation where the mouse is concerned…" She trailed off, a bit embarrassed about her Disney obsession, but really? Why should she be? Grown women could love rodents as well. Right?

"Yeah, I'm sure you do! Finish the story!" Seth rubbed his hands up and down her back, thankful that she believed him.

"So I showed her the picture of us wearing our mouse ears in front of Cinderella's Castle." She waited for his reaction, making sure he knew which picture she meant.

"Oh, yeah. I remember that picture."

"Well, she took one look, and her whole face lit up. She said you must love me a lot to be willing to wear those." She looked up at him, loving the look in his brown eyes. "That's when I thought maybe you hadn't been lying after all. I know Bob never would have been caught dead in those silly mouse ears, but you put them on every morning for a week to show you cared. You were telling me you loved me every time you put those silly things on your head." She stood on tiptoe and kissed his chin, barely able to reach it.

He grinned. "I'm so glad you realized it. I also tell you I love you every time I kiss you." He leaned down and pressed his lips to hers. "Every time we make love. Every time I ask for your opinion. I do love you, Michelle Strempel."

"The name is Henderson. Michelle

Henderson."

He raised an eyebrow. "Even professionally?"

"Especially professionally. My students need to know I'm yours."

"Why didn't you believe me to start with?" he asked.

She sighed. "I've believed for years that it's not possible for a man to really love me. Not the kind of love I read about in romance novels at least. Not the kind of love that would make a man spend the rest of his life with just one woman, loving her and no other."

"Why?"

She shrugged. "Because no one ever had, I think. I don't know. I was just so convinced of it. There's a line in *Cyrano de Bergerac* that says, 'My friend, I have my bitter days, knowing myself to be so ugly, so alone...' I always felt that way. We read *Cyrano* in high school, and I felt like it fit me well. Like no one would ever be able to look at me with love. I didn't have the big nose, but I felt hideous just the same. So I convinced myself that any man showing me any attention wanted something. They wanted a free tutor. They wanted someone to babysit. Something! I think that's why I went out with Bob. Because I thought I'd never find anyone who cared for me. When he told me he loved me, I never believed him. I thought I should play along though, if I didn't want to spend the rest of my life alone."

He shook his head in amazement. "Do you want to know what my first thought was when I saw you walking down the aisle toward me?"

"What?"

"That you were the most beautiful woman

I'd ever seen, and I couldn't believe you'd had to resort to a matchmaker. I couldn't believe you were really going to be mine." He stroked her cheek with one finger. "Michelle, you're an incredible, beautiful woman with a heart for people. How on earth could you think you were unlovable?" It broke his heart to realize she didn't think as much of herself as he did of her.

She shrugged, looking up into his eyes. "I just always thought that. You've convinced me otherwise, though. There's just something about the way you look at me that makes me feel so loved."

"You are. You are the most loved woman on the planet. Please don't ever forget that." He held her close, kissing her softly. "I thank God every day for sending you to me. I love you. More than I could ever say."

She sighed contentedly, pulling his head

down for another kiss. "I love you right back, Seth Henderson. I want to spend the rest of my life loving you."

"You really don't have a choice," he said with a grin. "I'm keeping you."

Epilogue

Dr. Lachele pushed end on the call with Michelle Henderson, thrilled to have brought love into another couple's world. She didn't have time to bask in the glory of a good match though.

She had received a call from a doctor in Northlake, Texas, who needed a bride. But who to match up with him? She picked up his picture and stared at it for a moment. "Who do you need?" she asked him.

She'd already done his preliminary testing, and she was sure she could place him. Seth's twin brother, a doctor in a suburb of Fort Worth, Texas. "I don't think I've found your perfect woman yet, but I will. I promise you, I'll have you married within the next six months."

Slade Henderson would be her next project. She was sure to find him someone perfect!

Made in the USA
Coppell, TX
18 October 2025